DANGEROUS SUMMER

Dangerous Summer

Carolyn Hart

INTEGRATED MEDIA
NEW YORK

ISBN: 979-8-3372-0395-9

This edition published in 2026 by Open Road Integrated Media, Inc.
180 Maiden Lane
New York, NY 10038
www.openroadmedia.com

To my parents
Doris Akin Gimpel and Roy William Gimpel

DANGEROUS SUMMER

1

THE JOURNEY BEGINS

The flight-call burst from the loudspeaker, and her mother and father looked at each other. Nan knew that if she showed the slightest qualm, they'd call the whole thing off and, one way or another, personally escort her to her grandmother's. But it wasn't the journey she feared. It was the long, lonely winter that lay at its end. So she grinned more widely, grabbed her book (as if she could read on her first trip in an airplane) and jumped up from the slick brown leather chair.

"Come on, slowpokes," she commanded lightly. "It's time to see the world traveler on her way." Turning her back, she started across the shiny terrazzo floor of the waiting room. She forced another bright smile and chided, "Now don't begin to worry about your little girl. I couldn't be in safer hands. I heard you say so yourselves."

"That's right, Moira," her father said to her mother. "Mrs. Stimson can take care of Nan."

"I know she will, James," her mother answered. She hesitated, then added uncertainly, "It's just that it's so far—and all the other students on the tour will be older. . . ."

Nan paused to draw her mother's arm through her own. "Mother," she said gently, "it isn't a prison sentence! No one ever planned a more fabulous year for a fifteen-year-old girl. And you're marvelous to do it. Now, you and Daddy will ruin your whole stay in Ethiopia if you sit around worrying about me."

They stopped beside the gate. Passengers were filing through the opening in the chain-link fence to board the massive jetliner, gleaming in the early morning sunlight. The slender, dark-haired girl hugged her mother hard. "I'll miss you both," she said. "A year is a long time, but we'll all have so much fun. Thanks for being such wonderful parents."

Mrs. Russell, her eyes suspiciously bright, smiled at her daughter. "Do have a good year, Nan," she urged, her Scottish burr accent still strong, even after all her years in the Midwest. "And take care, my dear."

Wordlessly, the girl kissed her mother, then turned to hug her tall father a moment. He murmured anxiously into her straight chestnut-brown hair, "It is all right, isn't it?"

She stepped back and smiled up at him. "Of course it is, Daddy."

The last call for her flight sounded. Almost all the passengers had boarded. Taking a firm grip on her book, her purse, and her courage, Nan cried, "Good-bye, good-bye. It's going to be a great summer. I'll write and you do, too."

She turned away swiftly. Showing her ticket to the attendant, she passed through the gate and walked quickly toward the plane. She climbed the steep steps of the ramp, and, at the top, paused to look back one last time. Her parents stood by the fence, waving farewell, but looking very forlorn. Sunlight glinted in her mother's auburn hair, but Nan knew that tears filmed the usually cool and steady blue eyes. Her father's lean, lanky frame hunched stiffly forward. The girl swallowed her own sadness, swung her hand with the book in a cheerful arc, then turned and walked into the plane.

She found a seat by a rather wilted young mother traveling with a small baby and a toddler. In the excitement of strapping on her seat belt and retrieving her book from the sticky grasp of the little boy, she was too occupied to feel the pangs of homesickness that had threatened to overwhelm her all morning. But as the plane taxied slowly up the field, she craned her neck for a final glimpse of her parents—and she felt unhappy and frightened.

The powerful jets roared, and the plane seemed to strain and stretch. Slowly it began to move and then suddenly it was streaming up the runway. As it pulled away from the ground and began to climb, she peered over the heads of her seat-mates, but the airport was gone in a flash—and with it, the world she knew. The girl slumped back into her seat with a sigh and began to unfasten her seat belt. She was on her way—for a whole year.

Blinking very hard, she vowed to herself, "I won't cry. I won't! It's idiotic to be homesick when you've just barely left, and, besides, by next week home won't be anywhere!"

That was the heart of the matter. Oh, the house would be there, but not her parents. Nan was glad she had smiled all the way, because her father really was excited about his project in Ethiopia: searching for minerals in a country whose mineral deposits were virtually untouched. And her mother was looking forward to seeing Africa and visiting some of the new archaeological excavations.

It was just bad luck that her father's work would be in a remote area far from an American school. Instead, she would spend the year in Edinburgh with her grandmother. And this dismayed her almost as much as the prospect of a year away from her mother and father. Not the idea of being with her grandmother. When the elderly Scotswoman visited America five years ago, her gentle wit had enchanted Nan. No, what Nan dreaded was attending a strange school where the students would think her strange too.

She could feel the hot tears threatening to fall, but she shook her head determinedly and decided to stop worrying about the long winter and concentrate on the summer ahead. It, at least, would be wonderful.

Her eyes cleared as she thought of her father and mother. At first they had planned to send her directly to Scotland, but her father had said thoughtfully, "It's a shame to be abroad for an entire year and not do any traveling."

"But, James," her mother objected, "Grandma isn't up to traveling over the continent. And I don't think we should ask her."

"Of course not," he replied. "I was thinking more along the line of a tour with other students."

Nan saw to it that the idea wasn't forgotten. Finally her parents had decided it would be all right because an old friend, Mrs. Stimson, was chaperone of a study tour.

And here she was, en route to New York City to join Laramie European Tour Number 586. She would sail for Europe tomorrow. Pulling out the well-thumbed brochure describing the trip, she gazed in wonder at the list of cities. She had read about all of them, but now she'd actually see Paris and London, Rome and Vienna.

Looking to the future, she managed a small smile. Her mother and father were so funny! They were so concerned about her touring Europe at fifteen. They didn't realize her hesitation wasn't over the tour; it was the long winter in Edinburgh that worried her. She grinned. Poor old parents. What could be safer than a guided, chaperoned tour? Snuggling down in her seat, she took out a map provided by the agency and began to trace the fabulous journey that lay ahead.

When the jet landed at Dulles International Airport near Washington, D.C., Nan watched the debarking passengers with interest. It seemed odd that she would see the capitals of most European countries long before she visited her own. However, she and her parents planned to stop over on their way home next June, after they joined her in Scotland. Next year. . . . She quickly bent back to her map. Well, even if she didn't have an idea in the world what life would be like in Edinburgh, she was sure of the future for the next ten weeks. It was all in her itinerary.

But not quite everything was in the itinerary the slender girl studied with such absorption. . . .

As the plane carrying Nan lifted into the sky, heading toward New York, an official of the Central Intelligence Agency sat in his Washington office. He was slowly rereading a message his secretary had just placed before him. A frown creased his forehead, and he asked her, "Do we have a file on this Dr. Neal Yates?"

"No, sir. I checked before I brought the message."

"Hmm. Try the FBI," he directed. "If there's anything to this, we've got to warn him."

She left the room and the man studied the information forwarded by an agent in Berlin. He removed his glasses and rubbed his eyes. Always so many loose ends, so many dangling threads. He looked again at the report. They must find this Dr. Neal Yates, American, address unknown, and very tactfully suggest that he shouldn't go to Europe this summer. Why? We have this report. . . . No, it isn't substantiated. No, sir, we can't require you to cancel your trip. But for your own good. . . .

There might be something to it or there might not, he thought. He would order some discreet inquiries, but probably they'd come to nothing. He couldn't afford to spare an agent on such an insubstantial tip. Absently he reached for his cold pipe and chewed on its stem. The threat was bizarre, off-key. It didn't make sense. But he'd been in this business for a long time, and the little message tingled the nerves at the base of his neck. On the face of it, he wouldn't be justified in assigning an agent, but perhaps there was a way out. They would have to move very fast. A thoughtful light in his eyes, he began methodically to fill his pipe.

While a plan was evolving in this small Washington office, Nan's plane neared New York. Passengers began to replace magazines in the seat racks and rustle expectantly. The girl looked through her window as the captain announced points of interest: the Hudson River, Manhattan, Long Island. The jet curved, dipped and landed. The first step of her journey was complete.

Startled by the size and bustle of the airport, she finally located the airline's baggage center and claimed her luggage. She waved away a porter. The tour agency had been most emphatic—each traveler had to carry what he brought and she might as well get used to it now. She lifted her two medium-weight brown suitcases and hurried outside into the sweltering heat of a June day in New York. The cab stands surged with people. She kept losing her place in line, but a sympathetic cabbie finally yelled, "Hey, you there, the little girl in the yellow dress. You're next."

Gratefully she climbed into the rear seat and directed him to the Women's Residential Hall at Columbia University, the gathering point for Laramie Tour members.

The dormitories were a little disappointing to Nan, so gray

and unimaginative compared with the shiningly modern living areas at the university where her father taught. And the crowded streets with their old, dingy buildings were different also. She checked in at the desk of the dormitory and inquired about other members of her tour.

"They've been arriving all day long, Miss Russell." The receptionist glanced down at a pad. "All Laramie Tour members are to meet in the main lounge at eight in the morning."

Nan thanked her for the room key, picked up her luggage and walked to the elevator. She watched the indicator above the doors moving slowly down. The elevator opened to release a chattering group of girls who appeared to be old friends.

"Terri, if you get seasick, you'll have to find another cabinmate," a bouncy redheaded girl said.

"Who, me? Seasick? Listen, I've got—"

Nan wondered if they were going to be part of her tour. They looked like fun. Happily she stepped into the elevator and punched the button for the fourth floor. When the doors slid open, she glanced at her key. Room 432. She moved down the linoleum-covered hall with its antiseptic yet dusty smell, counting numbers as she went. Here it was.

The door stood open to a box of a room, furnished with twin beds, two desks and two straight-backed chairs. On one bed a suitcase lay open, and bending over it was a slender girl in a blue silk dress with the most stunning ash blonde hair Nan had ever seen. She tapped on the open door. The other girl turned and gazed stonily at her.

"I'm Nan Russell," she offered a little hesitantly.

The blonde girl nodded, unsmiling. "I suppose you're my roommate for the tour," she said. "Well, come in. I don't bite." And she turned back to her suitcase.

Nan stood there, a little at a loss. She'd wondered what her roommate would be like, but never in a million years had she expected to be greeted as enthusiastically as a cold shower in January. Her dark-brown eyes blinking nervously, she crossed to the other bed and dumped her luggage.

The blonde girl regarded her coolly. "My name's Leslie Whitaker," she said. "I'm from Arlington, Virginia."

"I live in Lawrence, Kansas," Nan responded as she began to take out what she'd need that night. Her roommate curled up on the other bed and watched her silently. Finally there was nothing more to unpack, and Nan forced herself to meet the steady gaze of Leslie's violet eyes.

It was Nan who broke the lengthening silence. "Have you met any of the other tour members yet?"

"No," said the blonde girl. "I imagine we will soon enough." She paused, her face marred by a sullen frown.

Oh brother, Nan thought, what a ball this is going to be! Suddenly she realized her own expression must reflect her sour thoughts—and this wasn't a day to be unhappy! Five dozen surly roommates weren't going to ruin the greatest adventure she would ever have. She snapped her suitcases shut and picked up her purse.

"Where are you going?" the girl asked unexpectedly.

Nan looked at her, considered for a moment, then answered, "I've never been to New York and I have a half day to spend. I'm going to the Metropolitan Museum of Art."

Leslie's eyebrows flicked up in disdain as she swung off her bed. "I think I'll go shopping." She slipped a handbag over her arm and walked lithely to the door. At the threshold, she paused and suggested, "You'd better wear flats." Then she was gone.

2

THE DARK-HAIRED WOMAN

Nan strolled through the great corridors of the museum, stopping first in one gallery and then another. She stood for a long time before Greek statues with flowing lines and graceful simplicity. And she'd always remember the flaming beauty of canvases by Titian and Tintoretto, the sixteenth century Italian masters. At every turn, a new treasure awaited.

But in the famous Egyptian section of the museum, she dropped wearily onto a marble bench tucked in an alcove and wriggled her feet. She had a sudden flash of warm feeling for Leslie. Thank goodness she'd followed her advice and worn flats. She could imagine how her feet would ache if she'd remained in heels.

And then she heard the sharp, hurried tip-tap of someone approaching the gallery in high heels. She was curious to see who'd be wearing them, for she had seen only a few persons in her wandering in the museum the whole afternoon—two nuns shepherding a group of children, an artist with an easel painstakingly copying the work of another painter.

A trim, well-dressed woman in her early twenties came in view. Her black hair, worn straight in a short Italian cut, fit her head like a shiny cap of ebony. She looked up and down the gallery, her gaze sweeping the marble benches in the center of the room. She didn't glance toward the girl's alcove or its twin midway down the chamber. Intrigued, Nan watched as the young woman checked her watch with a worried look. Not once did she look at the sarcophagus near which she stood or at the other relics of the civilization which existed so long ago. Instead, she paced nervously up and down, six steps forward, six steps back.

Obviously, the girl decided, she wasn't here to admire Egyptian art. Nan studied her with interest. Her well-cut sheath dress was shell-pink, a hard shade to look well in, but it suited her ivory complexion and brought out the dark sheen of her hair. She was almost beautiful, although her sharply planed face looked too severe. The girl began to imagine reasons for this attractive woman to be waiting so impatiently on a hot June day near a stone coffin in the Metropolitan Museum. Perhaps she and her fiance had quarreled and this was to be a crucial encounter. Perhaps she was to meet . . .

Nan and the woman heard the footsteps at the same moment—the heavy, unhurried tread of a man nearing the gallery. The woman lifted her head and turned toward the hall, her face very still as the measured steps grew louder, nearer.

Leaning forward a little, curious to watch this meeting, Nan blinked in sudden surprise. The young woman who had listened so intently, so conscious of the man's approach, abruptly started to concentrate on the descriptive plaque on the tomb.

She didn't look up when a middle-aged man in a crumpled brown suit entered the chamber, his head bowed as he read what appeared to be a guidebook. He stopped before a funeral frieze depicting a warrior's life. The woman was still immersed in her study of the sarcophagus. It didn't have that much to offer. Nan felt puzzled. This was no lovers' meeting. But what was it? She watched uneasily, drawing back into the shadow of her alcove.

The man and woman might each have been alone in the gallery. Moving away from the tomb painting, the man stood for a moment before a remnant of a sculptured head. Finally he walked to the center of the chamber, sat down on a marble bench and began to make notes in his guidebook, glancing occasionally at the sculpture. He laid the booklet down, frowned as if in deep thought, then rose and returned to the frieze. The booklet remained on the bench. After a long moment he turned toward the exit and slowly walked out.

Nan's eyes swung back to the woman, still bending over the stone coffin. She knew that the dark-haired woman was concentrating on the dwindling echo of that heavy tread. Abruptly the woman straightened up and strolled toward the archway to the main hall, pausing at each exhibit for a moment. Moving gracefully alongside the bench where the man had sat, she slowed down for an instant. When she was past, the booklet was no longer there. Her pace quickened. She was at the exit and gone.

Nan stood up from her bench. The strange encounter seemed to chill the room. She shivered, but perhaps she was only tired. It had been a long time since she boarded that jet in Kansas City.

A little hurriedly, she walked toward the exit. You do see all sorts of things in New York City, just as she had read.

The sharp tip-tap of high heels brought her up short. The woman was returning. Nan almost turned back to the alcove, then stopped with a jerk. That was silly. After all, it was a public museum.

When the slender young woman clicked into the chamber,

she saw Nan immediately. Her swinging gait checked perceptibly. For only an instant she looked startled, and then her expression smoothed into blankness. Without another glance at the girl, the woman walked directly to the tomb, picked up a pair of pale pink gloves nestling there, turned on her heel and left.

Nan hesitated for a moment, then determinedly walked toward the exit. But she turned in the opposite direction from the fading click of high heels. What a spooky performance! she thought.

All the way back to the dormitory, she re-ran the odd scene in her mind. It was hot and empty when she let herself into the room. Suddenly she wished that she had gone shopping with Leslie. Even her company would have been lots better than the uncomfortable memory of that strange meeting.

She sat down on the mattress of her bed and absently ruffled the faded chenille spread. What made it such an eerie interlude? she asked herself. It wasn't only that the woman had ignored the man, after having listened so hard to his approaching footsteps. After all, she could have been expecting someone else, not the man at all. But she'd picked up the little booklet that he left behind on the bench!

Okay, so she had picked up a discarded booklet, that's no crime, Nan argued with herself. Maybe she didn't like litterbugs. Maybe she simply wanted to read it.

It wasn't that simple, and Nan knew it. The man and woman had been so aware of each other. Hidden in the alcove, Nan could almost have reached out and touched that awareness.

They'd met to exchange that leaflet. And all the subterfuge didn't make any sense at all unless the leaflet was very important.

Nan swung off the bed. Should she report the incident? She fought against the idea. Report it to whom, for heaven's sake?

She stared blankly out the window. She wouldn't know whom to tell. And what little she'd seen couldn't help anybody anyway. She was determined to push down the nagging thought that she could at least tell the tour leader.

She moved back to the bed and drew the map of Europe from her purse. Her mind was made up. She was not going to get involved. After all, no law had been broken by that odd couple—as far as she knew. A summer of fun lay before her. She would only complicate things for herself if she tried to take her tale to the authorities, and she wasn't going to let anything interfere with her marvelous summer.

When the alarm shrilled at six the next morning, a muffled moan rose from Leslie's bed. Nan flailed about with her arm, trying to hush the insistent clang and then realized where she was and why. With a whoop she pushed back her covers, grabbed the clock, and began to sing the old camp song, "It's time to get up, it's time to get up . . ."

"Must you be so nauseatingly cheerful? Do you do this every morning?" Leslie poked her head out from under the pillow.

"Every morning," she said gleefully. "At home they call me the happy morning warbler. I greet the dawn with a song."

"Oh, knock it off." An unwilling grin crept to the other girl's lips.

Nan grinned back. They'd eaten together the evening before, and finally the blonde girl relaxed and enjoyed herself. Perhaps she had been tired or homesick earlier in the day. Anyway, Nan wasn't going to waste a minute of her trip worrying about her roommate's changeable disposition.

She swung her legs over the edge of the bed and sat for a moment, a happy smile lighting up her slender, heart-shaped face.

Leslie gave a small sigh. Her violet eyes were a little forlorn, and she asked, "You're very happy, aren't you?"

Nan gazed at her in surprise. "Happy?" she repeated. "I'm delirious. This very day, this very morning, we'll board a boat and be on our way to Europe. This is the biggest adventure I've ever had. Of course, I'm happy!"

The unhappy look that had begun to knot Leslie's brows faded a little, then disappeared altogether. "You're right," she said. "It is a grand adventure and nothing should ruin it."

Nan stared at her, puzzled. Some sort of crisis had been reached. She knew instinctively that her roommate needed action, not talk. Jumping up, she caught the other girl's hand and said, "What are we doing, just sitting here? Let's get this day on the road!"

Not more than ten minutes later, the girls, breathless from their quick showers and spilling over with excitement, started down for breakfast.

As they entered the cafeteria, Nan pointed out the six girls she'd noticed leaving the elevator yesterday. "Look, do you suppose they're part of our group?"

"I'll bet they are," Leslie said.

As the roommates passed near the group's table, they heard snatches of the conversation.

". . . and my sister said you can buy the most beautiful sweaters in Vienna. . . ."

"But in London there's a store. . . ."

". . . the china is so lovely, and Mother said. . . ."

As they moved on, Nan remarked, "It sounds like a shopping trip to me."

The blonde girl laughed. "Oh well, let them enjoy it their way and we'll be the ones who look at the castles instead of the cashmeres."

Nan felt a warm sense of companionship for Leslie. If her moody roommate could keep on smiling, the journey would be doubly fun.

After a quick breakfast of sweet rolls and coffee, the girls hurried to the main lounge for the first meeting of their tour.

The large room was crowded with couches, easy chairs and coffee tables. The green drapes were closed, and the room seemed a little dim and musty. In the wintertime it would surge with vitality, filled with coeds reading or studying, chatting quietly or daydreaming. But now it was deserted except for one corner where excited teenagers were gathering.

The girls drew near, a little shyly. Dominating one huge couch were the six girls they'd noticed earlier. Other boys and girls perched on chair arms or lounged against the wall.

One boy, with amused gray eyes and a wheat-colored crew cut, sat a little apart. The girls settled on a couch opposite his chair. He grinned at them.

"Hi," he said. "I'm Jack O'Neill. Are you part of the Laramie Tour?"

The girls nodded in unison and introduced themselves.

"Have you met the professor who's going to lead the tour?" Nan inquired.

"Yes," Jack replied, "He stayed at the men's dorm with us last night. His name is Dr. Neal Yates and he seems like a good guy—maybe a little serious for my taste. He teaches European history at Stanford. I'll be a freshman there this fall. Here he comes now."

Dr. Yates strode across the lounge. He was a husky, broad-shouldered bear of a man, yet he moved with the grace of an athlete.

He's so big, Nan thought, and so young! She smiled a little to herself. The others probably wouldn't think so, but to her he looked like a graduate student. And he probably had been one not too long ago, she decided as he drew nearer.

A wide grin on his tanned face, the professor introduced

himself. “I know you’re all very excited this morning, and I’m just as eager to begin as you are,” he told them. “This will be my first journey abroad too. I know we’ll enjoy studying history where it actually happened.” He paused and added in an oddly measured tone, “I wouldn’t miss it for anything.” For an instant a grimly determined expression hardened his face. Then the wide smile was back in place. “Now, have all of you met? No? Okay, we’ll go round-robin.”

Nan tried to pin names to faces, but there were too many. It wasn’t hard to remember the red-headed and freckle-faced twins, Pat and Polly Brock, or Jack O’Neill, the boy who’d introduced himself earlier. She knew everyone would get acquainted aboard ship, so she sat back, studied her new friends and liked what she saw.

Boys would certainly be at a premium, though! There were only six of them to the eleven girls.

After the last boy, Johnny West, introduced himself, Dr. Yates said, “Fine. Everyone’s here except Mrs. Stimson, our guide.” He glanced at his watch. “She should be with us any minute. I’ll just run through our procedure for boarding. . . .” He broke off, looked through the archway and called out, “Are you looking for the Laramie Tour?”

Nan turned to look toward the entrance. Standing there was the black-haired woman who had acted so mysteriously at the museum.

3

WHAT HAPPENED TO MRS. STIMSON?

For the barest instant their eyes met and held. Then the woman looked past Nan to Dr. Yates, her face again a smooth mask.

Nan was nonplussed. Maybe she was wrong—but, no, she wasn't! In that first moment their recognition had been mutual. She leaned forward as the woman spoke to the professor.

"My name is Karen Mitchell," she said in a cool, composed voice. "Mrs. Stimson, the agency chaperone, is ill. I'm her replacement." She opened her bag. "Here's the information about boarding the ship, currency requirements in France, and booklets with detailed descriptions of the planned tours."

The young professor looked surprised. "Ill? But she seemed quite all right when I saw her yesterday. It must have been quite sudden."

"It was," the woman replied after a moment's hesitation. "A heart attack, I think."

"I'm sorry to hear that," he said slowly. "However, if you have all the information—"

"I've been thoroughly briefed by the agency," Miss Mitchell said crisply, "and I have everything well in hand."

Nan's puzzlement changed to concern. A heart attack could be so serious. She had to find out more about it. She waited impatiently as the guide outlined the boarding procedure.

The woman paused and glanced at her watch. "If there aren't any questions, I suggest we start right away."

Nan's hand shot up.

The guide's face stiffened. "Yes?"

"Do you know anything definite about Mrs. Stimson's condition?" the girl asked.

The woman shook her head, and then her gaze swept the group. "If there aren't any more questions, I suggest that everyone get his luggage and report back to the lounge in fifteen minutes. We'll then proceed to the harbor."

"Gee, I haven't finished packing!" Polly Brock squealed.

"Neither have I!" Pat echoed. "Let's hurry."

In an instant the group splintered, surging for the hallway. Nan was swept along, but questions swirled in her mind. She hesitated at the door. Leslie tugged impatiently on her hand. "What are you waiting for? It's time to go."

Nan looked at the telephone booth across the hall. She wouldn't be put off by the guide. Glancing back at the lounge, she saw Miss Mitchell talking to the professor, her back toward the exit.

The girl made up her mind. "I have to make a phone call. I'll join you upstairs."

Leslie looked at her curiously, but said nothing. "Sure thing. See you in a minute."

Nan hurried across the hall. She stopped, dismayed by the

sturdy rack beside the booth. How many phone books did New York City have? Quickly she flipped open the top one. Brooklyn. Oh, that made sense. A directory for each of the city's boroughs. Pulling down the Manhattan volume, she turned to the L's and ran her finger down the page, Lam-, Lap-, Lar-, Laramie Tour Agency—OX5-6002. She stepped into the booth, inserted a coin, and dialed.

On the third ring a well-modulated voice answered. "Laramie Tour Agency. May I help you?"

"Yes, please. Could you give me some information about one of your tour leaders, Mrs. Emily Stimson?"

"Who is speaking?" The voice inquired abruptly after a sharp, short pause.

"My name is Nan Russell. Mrs. Stimson's an old friend of my parents, Dr. and Mrs. James Russell. Since she isn't going to lead the tour, I wanted to find out how she is."

"Are you on Tour 586?" the receptionist asked.

"Yes."

The voice surged briskly through the receiver. "I'm very sorry, but I'm afraid you won't be able to speak to Mrs. Stimson. Perhaps on your way back through New York in September, you could call us again. I know Miss Mitchell will be a satisfactory guide, and I certainly wish you a *bon voyage*."

Sensing something strange, Nan asked, "Where *is* Mrs. Stimson?"

The silence wasn't long, but it added to her growing conviction that something was wrong.

"Mrs. Stimson is on her way south, I believe," the receptionist replied. "Some sort of family emergency."

The connection broke. Nan held the receiver for a moment, then slowly hung it up. In her mind's eye, she could see a well-manicured hand depressing the telephone cradle bar. Her lips tightened, and she reached for her wallet. Darn. Plenty of pennies, but no nickels or dimes.

A light knock sounded on the glass of the folding door. She turned around and looked into Miss Mitchell's cool green eyes. The tour leader's gaze dropped to the telephone rack. On top sat the Manhattan directory, open at the L's. Nan took a deep breath and pushed open the door.

For a moment the guide and the girl regarded each other warily. Suddenly Nan was angry. She liked things to be clear-cut. Anger made her bold. "I called the tour agency," she said.

Miss Mitchell raised her eyebrows in mild surprise. "That really isn't necessary, Miss—"

"Nan Russell," Nan said crisply.

"Miss Russell, if you have any questions about the tour, I can answer them."

"I called about Mrs. Stimson." The girl hesitated, then continued in a challenging tone. "They didn't seem to know about her heart attack."

The woman's face was very still, and then she shrugged lightly. "I don't suppose the receptionist knows." Her voice was as bland as custard.

Nan flushed. She didn't know how to handle this. She couldn't very well call the woman a liar. The guide broke the hostile silence. "Do you have your bags in the lobby?"

"No," she said. She moved to step past the woman but stopped abruptly.

"Did you enjoy the Egyptian collection?" she asked. And she almost smiled at the guide's soft, quick intake of air. That had startled her, all right!

"Collection?" the woman repeated slowly and shook her head. "What collection? You must have me confused with someone else. You'd better hurry. I see some of the students arriving in the lounge."

The guide turned away and crossed the hall to the meeting place, her high heels tapping on the marble floor. Nan remembered watching that same graceful walk—in the Egyptian room of the Metropolitan Museum.

The girl shook her head in anger. She'd certainly made a mess of things. All the way to her room, she tried to sort it out. First, what had happened to Mrs. Stimson? The telephone call hadn't solved anything. Only one point was sure—the new tour leader not only behaved peculiarly in museums, she lied also. She most certainly *had* been in the museum and she'd denied it! Someone, either the guide or the receptionist, was lying about Mrs. Stimson. Or at least one of them was mistaken.

She paused at the door of her room. The truth of it was, she was hopelessly confused. But there was something wrong about Miss Mitchell, and she must tell someone. She thought of Dr. Yates with relief. And then she realized that she couldn't tell him. Miss Mitchell would just deny the whole thing!

Nan could hear it all now. "Museum? Of course not, Dr. Yates." Her voice would be cool and composed. "I can't imagine why the girl is making this up, but some teenagers. . . ."

Nan gave up. What a mess! But it wasn't her mess! Why should she get involved? It wasn't any concern of hers what the guide did or whether Mrs. Stimson was traveling south or whether she was sick. She'd made an effort to find out what had happened to Mrs. Stimson, and there wasn't anything else she could do, short of making a fool of herself. The only sensible thing was to forget it all.

She nodded her head as if to convince herself that she'd made the right decision and stepped inside the room. Leslie's cool, dry voice shook her from her reverie. "Is this a scene from *Eliza*

At the River? Or could it be *Oh Dearie Me, I've Forgotten My Toothbrush And I Know Not What To Do*?"

Nan flushed. "I wasn't being dramatic," she said stiffly. "I was thinking about something."

Leslie's teasing smile faded away, and she said gently, "Hey, don't be so sensitive. It was just a joke."

"I'm sorry," Nan apologized, annoyed at herself, and smiled. "I guess I'm a little excited. It isn't every day you leave for Europe."

"No, darling," Leslie replied in her gently mocking tone. "And you won't make it today if you don't hustle. We're due downstairs in two, I repeat, two minutes."

"Oh my gosh," Nan cried. Racing to her bed, she began to snap her suitcases, muttering unhappily when she discovered her shower cap beneath one bag. She reopened it, hurriedly tucked the cap on top, slammed the lid and was ready to go.

Her roommate watched from the doorway, an amused smile on her face. "I don't really think they'll leave without us." She paused, then continued with a grin. "But I don't suppose you want to take the chance."

Nan grinned back. Leslie, she decided, was going to be quite a roommate—if she could remember to keep her sense of humor.

When they reached the lounge, Miss Mitchell was dividing the travelers into taxi groups. Nan smiled when she and Leslie and Jack O'Neill were scheduled to ride together—until the guide added, "And I'll go with you three."

Nan hunched into her corner of the taxi, Miss Mitchell beside her. All the way to the pier, while Leslie and Jack chatted, the woman plied Nan with polite questions.

It must all appear very innocuous, Nan thought resentfully, just the sort of small talk a guide would make with a student. But she and Miss Mitchell knew that the questions weren't innocuous at all. Where was she from? Who were her parents? How old was she? Had she met Dr. Yates before?

Why didn't the woman leave her alone? But Nan knew with cold certainty why question followed probing question. She'd been in the Metropolitan Museum at the wrong time and in the wrong place.

All she wanted to do was enjoy her summer, and Miss Mitchell was not going to ruin it for her.

At the pier, Nan maneuvered Jack and Leslie to the front of the group when Pat Brock came bouncing up to Miss Mitchell with a question.

As they raced happily ahead, the cool breeze swept away the anger that had boiled within her during the cab trip. Miss Mitchell's persistent questions were pushed deep into her mind as she said excitedly, "Look, there's our boat!"

Jack groaned. "Oh no, mate," he deplored. "Lesson one from a fellow who grew up with the sea in his backyard. Never, never call a ship a boat. It's a grave insult to the queen of the ocean!"

Nan gave a sigh of happiness. "Boat or ship, she's beautiful." The *S.S. Constantine* was in full view now, her dark-blue hull gleaming in the sunlight. Next stop: Europe.

4

TOPSY-TURVY CLOTHES

Nan paused halfway across the gangplank to gaze at the harbor. Massive liners were moored one next to the other. Perky tugboats, dingy yet colorful, darted purposefully about, sure of their own importance. Not even the most majestic liner could enter or leave the port without the assistance of the small tugs. The most impressive skyline in the world gleamed brilliantly in the sunlight. And over everything lay the smell of the sea, the salty scent of adventure.

Jack gave her a gentle shove between her shoulders. "Madam," he said, mockingly polite, "you may enjoy the view aboard. Not that I object to your pausing, but I hear a mumur of discontent behind me."

She flashed an unrepentant smile. "I'm sorry, but have you ever seen anything so marvelous!" She moved forward again, stepping carefully because the chasm between the ship and the pier was very impressive and she had no desire to find out just how far down it was.

"I could let out a war whoop myself," Jack said. "And this is just the beginning."

Once on board, Nan and Leslie and their new friend made a complete circuit of the sun deck.

"The ship is as big as a football field!" Nan exclaimed when they paused to rest for a moment against the deck railing.

"Bigger," the boy informed them. "Just about twice as long. Come on, landlubbers, I'll take you on a guided tour."

"I'll have you know I'm as much a seaman as you are," Leslie protested. "I've sailed Chesapeake Bay from one end to the other."

"Peace, my children," Nan broke in. "You needn't worry, Jack. You can be as superior as you like with me because I've never even been in a rowboat."

"Can you swim?" Leslie inquired.

Nan directed a withering glance at her. "Kansas may be dry, but we do have swimming pools, thank you."

"All right, girls, no regional bickering. It's all aboard for a guided tour. We are now standing on the sun deck, ladies, facing the bow. On our starboard is the pier while to port lies the harbor."

"A tactful way of letting me know right from left, I take it?" Nan asked.

"Um, yes," Jack admitted. "And I suppose you can tell forward from aft?"

"That isn't *too* hard," she said.

The trio explored the ship while Jack kept up a running commentary. On the sun deck, they visited the wireless office, a writing room, and an immense lounge filled with overstuffed furniture. Climbing down steel stairs to the promenade deck, they wandered through two smoking rooms, the dining room, a restaurant, a bar, and two card rooms. They located the purser's office, which was somewhat like a small store, offering ointments, seasick pills, cigarettes, newspapers, magazines, candies, postcards, and foreign currency. A, B, and C decks contained more reading and writing rooms, and cabins, cabins, cabins.

When they reached the engine room, Leslie decided that they'd had enough exploring for the day. "We've already walked five miles!" she exclaimed, and urged her companions upward and onward to the snack bar. "I spotted one someplace, and if I don't have a Coke, I'm going to perish like a camel overdue at an oasis."

"It was on the sun deck," Jack announced smugly.

"I can see now," Leslie snapped, "that you're going to be an infuriating person to travel with."

"Don't insult him," Nan said. "Anybody who knows where we are after the endless miles we've trudged is valuable."

The boy grinned just a little patronizingly.

"It's sort of the same principle as taking good care of the compass when your great-aunt gives you one for Christmas," she continued. "You may need it someday."

"Gee, thanks," Jack said in mock injury.

They'd just reached the sun deck when the *Constantine*'s whistle blew a deep, reverberating rumble.

"Do you suppose—"Nan began.

"We're sailing!" Leslie cried.

They hurried to the railing for a farewell view of the shore. Tugs jockeyed for position around the liner, and slowly, slowly, the ship began to move. The deep-throated blast sounded again and again. The wind ruffled lacy white-caps on the dark water. Gulls squalled and dipped, intent on their pursuit of unwary fish. Nan leaned against the cool metal and watched the receding shoreline. It would be a long time before she saw it again.

As the *Constantine* slid past the Statue of Liberty, Nan looked up at the figure of the woman, dressed in a flowing robe and holding a torch. How many bewildered refugees had been welcomed to America by that torch, the girl wondered. And now she was sailing away from that symbol of freedom to France, the country from which it had come so long ago.

More quickly than seemed possible, New York was a misty smudge on the horizon.

"I guess I have mixed emotions," Nan said finally in a quiet voice. "I won't be back for a whole year."

Her companions looked at her in surprise.

"A year?" the boy asked.

She nodded, a tight lump in her throat. She decided she couldn't start a grand adventure in a weepy spirit, so she forced a smile, took each by an arm, and said, "Forward march to the snack bar and I'll tell you all about it."

They settled around a table with sandwiches and Cokes, and Nan explained about her parents' journey and her own final destination, Scotland.

"That's great," Jack said. "Just think, a whole year in Europe!"

Leslie looked sullen, but said nothing.

Nan sat quite still, a thoughtful expression on her face. "I hadn't thought about it quite like that, but you're right, even though I will have to admit I'm worried about school." She waved her hand when he started to interrupt. "Nope, I'll face the winter when it comes. Right now I'm concentrating on the tour. At least that's predictable. And now, roommate, we'd better start looking for our cabin. I have a feeling it'll take until dusk to find it."

"Right," Leslie agreed. "We'll see you at dinner, Jack. Which sitting do we have, by the way?"

He pulled out the card bearing his cabin number, and said, "It's the first sitting, six-thirty."

"You know," Nan said as they walked uncertainly down the passageway, "this motion is sort of like walking on one of those movable floors in a fun house, only a lot easier."

"Yes," Leslie said. "Unless we run into a storm."

Their cabin was at the end of a narrow corridor. The steel door was painted a creamy white. Leslie grasped the handle, but paused before turning it.

"I imagine we have some cellmates, so should we burst right in?"

Nan shrugged. "Let's compromise. Open it, but slowly, so we won't seem rude."

The door swung inward to reveal a plump, white-haired woman comfortably ensconced in what turned out to be the cabin's only chair.

"Hello," she greeted them cheerfully, her bright brown eyes shining with gaiety. "I'm Amanda Royston. Are you my cabin-mates? Come in, come in."

Introducing themselves, the girls moved toward their luggage while Mrs. Royston continued her chatter. ". . . and I decided I was just too old to walk around the decks any longer, although I assure you I won't monopolize our only chair. But it's going to be a wonderful trip, isn't it? Are you girls on a tour? I'm taking a sabbatical from my high school in Conway, Montana. I've been saving every penny for years. I teach history and I'm so looking forward to seeing Europe at last."

Leslie shot an amused but kind look at her friend.

When the talkative teacher paused, Nan asked, "Have you met our other cabinmate?"

"Not yet," the white-haired woman said. "Her things were already here when I came down." She gestured toward the lower bunks. On one sat two sensible-looking cases of brown leather. On the other lay a fleecy shawl. "But she'll probably be in soon."

The teacher talked about Conway, the ship, her sightseeing plans and her class. The girls took turns murmuring "Yes" and "Really" while they propped their cases on luggage stands bolted to the end of each double bunk.

The door of the cabin opened, admitting a tall, slender woman in gray tweeds with short-cropped salt-and-pepper hair.

"Hello," she said in a brisk voice. "I'm Rhoda Dawes, your fourth."

"Oh, a fourth," Mrs. Royston bubbled. "Do you play bridge?" Not waiting for an answer, she continued, "I'm Amanda Royston and these sweet young things are Leslie Whitaker and Nan Russell. They're just the age of my granddaughters."

"I'm glad to meet all of you," Miss Dawes said. "Are you on a tour?" She lifted the lid of her case and began to unpack methodically.

Nan decided that if Miss Dawes could successfully combine unpacking and conversation, so could she. Reaching in her purse, she drew out her luggage key, inserted it and twisted. When she tried to lift the lid, it wouldn't budge. Then she turned the key in the opposite direction, and the case opened easily.

How odd, she thought, as she listened absent-mindedly to Leslie describing their tour to Miss Dawes. The suitcase must have been unlocked the first time she turned the key. She remembered locking it after she'd put in her shower cap at the last moment, but now it wasn't on top of her pajamas where she'd tossed it in her hurry.

The girl stared at her open case, puzzled. For that matter, nothing was where she'd left it. Lingerie was crumpled in one corner. A hairbrush thrust itself rakishly between a nightgown and a blouse. She became suddenly aware that an interested silence had enveloped the cabin. She looked up to see her companions watching her curiously.

"What's wrong?" Leslie asked. "You look upset."

"I—it's my luggage." She pointed at the disarray. "I pack very neatly," she continued slowly. "You wouldn't think clothes would get jumbled being hoisted on the ship."

"They would not," Miss Dawes agreed.

"Why, how very peculiar," trilled Mrs. Royston, her face puckered with concern.

Nan turned to Leslie and asked, "You do remember, don't you? I put my shower cap in the very last thing. Because we were going to be late."

"That's right," her friend said.

"I put it right on top of my pajamas." She paused. "And now I found it on the very bottom of the suitcase."

There was a moment's silence.

Miss Dawes pushed her hand through her graying hair. "The answer's quite obvious," she suggested without emphasis. "Someone has been through your luggage. Check to see what's missing."

As Miss Dawes spoke, Mrs. Royston gave an excited squeal. "Perhaps all the luggage has been searched." She scurried to her cases, opened the nearest one and riffled through it, muttering, "Now did I put that letter in the side pocket or not? Oh dear, I'm not sure, but I really don't think anything is missing."

Her face drawn, Nan lifted out her clothing, straightening things as she went.

The garrulous teacher returned to the easy chair and announced, "I may have seen the culprit."

The girl jerked up her head to stare at the older woman.

Nodding like a plump little bird, Mrs. Royston continued, ". . . I *thought* she was coming out of our cabin as I walked up the corridor, but of course, I decided I was mistaken. Now I'm not so sure." And her bright brown eyes were sharp and observant.

"What did she look like?" Miss Dawes asked.

"Oh, she was young and very pretty—the blackest hair, in one of the short, straight cuts. And a very good figure."

Leslie shook her head. "It couldn't be her. That's Miss Mitchell, our guide. She was probably checking to be sure our luggage had arrived." She continued eagerly, "But we could ask her if she saw anyone."

"Oh, no!" Nan burst out. She bit her lip when the others turned toward her. "I mean, we shouldn't make a fuss about it. Nothing's missing."

Miss Dawes leaned against the aft bulkhead. "It's very curious, isn't it?" she mused. "Someone searches your luggage, but takes nothing. It makes one wonder who did it. . . ."

5

VOICES IN THE FOG

Nan felt cold inside. There was no need for her to wonder. She knew whose hands had explored her bags—and there was nothing she could do about it. She couldn't openly accuse the guide unless she were willing to carry it all the way and insist that Miss Mitchell was something other than what she seemed. But she didn't know what Miss Mitchell was! Any accusation would be pointless.

When Mrs. Royston proposed that they call the purser, Nan quickly interrupted. "No," she said flatly.

Her cabinmates looked a little startled at her vehemence. With a conscious effort, she smoothed the tension out of her voice. "Let's not bother. After all, nothing's missing. It might be just a practical joke. And I don't want to make trouble for the purser. There isn't really anything he can do. It would just cause trouble."

Nan was grateful when Miss Dawes came to her support. "The girl's right," she said. "Nothing's been taken, so perhaps it's best to let sleeping dogs lie." Mrs. Royston gave in reluctantly.

Nan looked unhappily at her rumpled clothing. "I think I'll unpack later."

Leslie searched her face, then glanced down at her watch. "Oh, it's almost three. And we're supposed to meet Polly and Pat for bridge. We'd better hurry."

It was news to Nan, but it offered an escape. And she wanted to get out of there as soon as possible. "Yes," she quickly agreed. "Let's hurry."

As they neared the main stairway, she asked, "When did the twins invite us to play cards?"

"They didn't." Leslie grinned. "But I thought you looked a little wild-eyed."

"Thanks," she said.

The girls settled in the main lounge on the promenade deck with a Scrabble board. "It doesn't make sense," Leslie ventured as she plumped down an X after a free E. "I mean, nothing being taken. Why should someone just want to see what you have with you?"

Nan avoided the question. Instead, she asked, "Is it okay to form a prefix?"

"What?" Leslie peered at the board. "Oh, I thought it was an A. Ax. Just a minute."

Nan unclenched one hand to rearrange her letters. Her mouth felt dry and her chest had a hollow feeling. She had no idea why Miss Mitchell had searched her bags.

Leslie glanced up. "Hey," she said with concern. "You're really upset. You even look frightened!"

Nan relaxed the muscles in her face and forced a half-smile. "I'm all right. It worries me, but let's stop wasting our time on the ship on something so . . . pointless."

Her roommate studied her for a moment, then nodded in agreement. "That's a deal. Let's get busy and meet some people. What's one searched suitcase, more or less?"

The afternoon flashed by in a cheerful mixture of introductions, shuffleboard, bridge, and talk. But, always, the thought of Miss Mitchell nagged at Nan. At dinner she took a careful look up the table. The guide certainly didn't look sinister! Dressed in a pale green silk dress, she was really lovely, Nan decided grudgingly. It seemed absolutely impossible to imagine her creeping into their cabin to paw through her luggage. Nevertheless, the suitcases had been searched!

But as the days flew by and Miss Mitchell paid no attention to her, Nan began to relax. She swam every morning until the third day out, when the air chilled and they needed sweaters and afghans to keep cozy in the deck chairs. She had beginner's luck at shuffleboard, winning third place in an impromptu tourney. And every night she and Jack and Leslie joined other young travelers in the snack bar on the sun deck to sing college songs and listen to the music of a rinky-tink piano.

It was the fourth night out when Nan yawned right in the middle of "Show Me the Way to Go Home" and decided she really should go to sleep. She thought yearningly of her comfortable upper bunk and the lulling motion of the ship that carried her into deep and dreamless slumber.

She stood up and began to wiggle out of the booth. "I'm calling it a night. I want to be my very sharpest at shuffleboard in the morning." And she smiled at Jack, whom she'd beaten by the narrowest margin that day.

"I'll walk you to your cabin," he offered. Nan gently pushed him back in his seat as he started to rise. "The others will never forgive me if you do. You're the only one who knows all the verses."

"That's right," cried Terri Quinn, the irrepressible leader of the group from Indianapolis. "Without him, we'd be reduced to a mere hum."

The boy laughed. "I know when I'm outnumbered. But I will see you at breakfast?"

"Right," she said, pulling on her sweater. "Staying a while yet, Leslie?"

Her friend nodded. "I'm a born night owl and this is the first time I've ever been able to indulge myself and sleep 'til noon. No wonder you're tired! You stay up late every night, but you always get up for breakfast. You should follow my example."

"You should follow mine," Nan countered. "Breakfast is great. And I'm not going to ruin my record in the morning. Good night, all."

She smiled as she walked over the swaying floor, not faltering once. She was beginning to get her sea legs. Laughing to herself, she pushed open the heavy wooden door and stepped out on the deck. Sea legs. They sounded like appendages on some crusty, seaweed-coated ocean animal.

The cold night air fluttered her hair and brought her sharply awake. She paused to breathe the briny, lettuce-crisp air. She could hear the swish of water as the *Constantine* cut steadily through the sea. The deck rose and fell, gently.

As her eyes became adjusted to the dark, she realized a heavy fog swathed the ship. Only a diffused golden haze marked the windows of the lounge about a hundred and fifty feet across the open deck. The snack bar sat by itself, not far from the bow of the ship.

Slowly, savoring the smell and taste of the night, she walked toward the prow. The railing at the ship's head felt wet and cold. She leaned against the metal barrier, exhilarated by the steady, plunging thrust of the ship. Finally she took one last deep breath. She realized she was cold. It was time to go below.

The fog was thicker now. She couldn't see anything clearly as she turned, not even the snack bar. She hesitated, unsure and a little uneasy. She clutched the rail and carefully began to feel her way toward midship and the lounge.

The foghorn was sounding with measured regularity. As she groped her way aft, the girl realized the dull note wasn't new. It must have begun while she was standing at the bow, absorbed in the foggy night.

Nan shivered as her hand slid along the slick, moist metal. Except for the deck beneath her feet and the rough boom of the horn, she was lost in a world of dark and swirling mist, far from any other human being. She began to hurry.

At first the voices seemed only a part of the desolate scene, an added nightmarish quality. And then she felt a quick surge of relief. Someone else was out on the shrouded deck. She immediately felt safer.

Peering ahead, she tried to locate the nearby speakers, but her eyes couldn't pierce the blanket of fog. And then she halted, startled. The man's voice was heavy with anger.

". . . known from the first. You needn't think you fooled me for long, Miss Mitchell—if that's your name. It's probably as bogus as everything else about you."

"My name is Mitchell," the woman said. Her cool reply accentuated the anger in the man's voice.

"You're certainly calm about it," he snarled. "But I suppose this sort of charade is nothing new to you."

There was no reply.

His tone was nothing short of venomous as he continued.

"I want to make one thing very clear to you—no one's going to kidnap me!"

Her voice was measured and dispassionate. "You're a fool, Dr. Yates." She paused, then added quietly, "But fortunately that's not my concern. Good night."

The woman's heels clicked sharply against the wooden deck as she walked away. Dr. Yates muttered something beneath his breath. Then a cigarette lighter clicked. Nan saw a small flash of flame about four feet away. The man began to move toward the center of the ship.

The girl leaned against the railing. Kidnap! The ugly word seemed to echo and re-echo on the lonely deck. Kidnap!

The night and the fog seemed frightening now. She longed for her small cubicle deep in the ship, with its solid double bunks and tan-colored walls.

She struck off in the direction Dr. Yates and Miss Mitchell had gone, too upset to be afraid.

She'd traveled about fifteen feet when the door to the snack bar swung open, with the tinkling sound of music and a flash of light. She could make it now. Moving steadily, she reached the lounge and rushed inside. Just a few of the dozens of tables were in use. Only the hardiest card players remained. Nan swung around—and looked directly into the watchful green eyes of Miss Mitchell.

Nan just stood there. She couldn't speak.

"Have you been walking on the deck?" the woman asked. "It's rather dangerous in such a heavy fog."

"No, no," the girl replied hastily. "I've been in the snack bar with most of our group."

"You look a little cold," the guide said.

Nan realized suddenly that her hair was damp and little droplets of moisture clung to her face. She dropped her eyes, stuttered, "Good night, Miss Mitchell," and moved away.

"Good night, Nan." The woman's soft voice followed her, "I wouldn't concern myself with anything but sightseeing and fun if I were you."

The girl stopped and turned about. Miss Mitchell's dark head was bent and she was studying her slender hands with absorption. Nan knew she didn't want to be standing there if the guide should look up. With a quick breath she flew across the room, her steps clattering loudly on the polished floor.

Nan had no recollection of her mad dash through the ship, rushing down the stairways, careening along the halls. She drew her first full breath when she reached the cabin. She waited a moment in the hall for her heart to stop its wild thumping, and quietly eased open the heavy door. The dim glow of a night light over the wash basins showed her that Mrs. Royston and Miss Dawes were asleep.

Thankfully, she went to her bunk and reached for her pajamas. She slipped them on, turned to the basin and brushed her teeth. As quietly as possible, she climbed up the little ladder to her soft bunk. Snuggling beneath two heavy wool blankets, she slowly began to get warm. But no matter how gently her bed rose and fell, sleep wouldn't come that night.

6

COMPLICATIONS!

Nan was absorbed in her thoughts as she walked up the carpeted main stairs the next morning. What should she do? And good grief, how could she decide when she wasn't even sure there was anything to be done! Her mind was a muddled mess. Without being aware of it, she plunked her hand from one gilded banister to the next.

Jack's laughing voice startled her, and she looked up.

"Hey, pal, are you practicing basic addition?"

She hesitated a moment, then laughed. "I *was* counting, wasn't I? Sometimes I frighten myself. I'll probably end up as woolgathering as my father."

"Is he really an absent-minded professor?"

"Not really. But Mother always takes care of all the practical things for him because he's usually in a fog about his papers or his overshoes or his pipe. He knows Mother will find them."

"They sound nice," Jack said.

"They are."

The boy asked, "Do I detect a touch of homesickness?"

She stiffened a little. "No, of course not. It's just that they've always been there, you know, when I wanted to talk to them."

"No serious talks permitted on vacation," he joked.

Though she was tempted to tell him the whole story, she decided quickly against it. Jack was kind and entertaining, but she knew he would think she was just an imaginative nitwit. So she smiled brightly and said, "No talks, but letters are all right, aren't they?"

"Permission granted," he said.

"Thanks. I'll write them after breakfast, but right now I'm starving."

They found a table to themselves in the sparsely-filled dining room, and Nan had to admit she felt much more cheerful after breakfast. But she didn't know how much of her contentment came from the tangy bacon and the light-golden omelet and how much from the presence of the boy across the table. She liked the crisp cut of his sandy hair, and the way a band of freckles marched haphazardly across his nose and the irreverent gleam in his eyes. They lingered over coffee until she said, "I must get that letter written."

"Okay, but when you finish, how about some shuffle-board?"

"I'd love it." She smiled.

She settled at a decorated desk in the writing room, pulled her fountain pen out of her purse, and drew some ship stationery from the front drawer.

The light in her eyes faded away. How should she begin? With her sense of uneasiness, almost of fear, concerning Miss Mitchell? No, that wouldn't make sense at all. First, she must organize everything that had happened—try to make some sort of pattern. Hesitantly, then more surely, her hand moved across the page. Finally she was satisfied with what she'd written. She sat back and studied her list of incidents.

1. The curious performance in the museum when Miss Mitchell ignored the man in the gallery, then retrieved the booklet he'd left behind.
2. Miss Mitchell's concern when she discovered Nan in the tour group.
3. The "mystery" of Mrs. Stimson. Did the older woman have a heart attack or . . . what?
4. The guide's denial that she'd been in the museum.
5. The search of Nan's luggage.
6. The frightening conversation between the guide and the professor, then the bland warning Miss Mitchell had given her.

The girl's satisfaction dwindled as she read. It might appear nebulous and insubstantial to anyone who didn't know her, but her mother and father knew her very well indeed. "Nan, dear, they'll be frightened silly," the girl told herself in disgust. She sat quite still as this realization seeped through her mind. Even worse, her parents would be doubly-worried because they'd be helpless to act.

Idly she began to doodle boxes and circles and funny long-tailed cats while her thoughts raced ahead. For the first time in her life, it would be wrong to confide in her parents! She studied this new realization very closely. She'd only cause them fear and uncertainty, and there was nothing they could do. If there were some sort of plot, it was directed against Dr. Yates, and apparently he was well aware of it. All her parents could accomplish, at great expense and effort, would be to remove her from the tour. And this wasn't what she wanted at all. No, she wanted to wash her hands of the whole affair, push it off on someone else.

Her dark-brown eyes narrowed in self-examination. The girl knew that she didn't want to be involved—but she couldn't walk away from the word "kidnap." It'd been easier to justify ignoring the odd scene in the museum and even the search of her suitcases. But now. . . .

She thoughtfully chewed on the end of her pen. Of course, Dr. Yates wasn't her responsibility. He was a grown man perfectly capable of taking care of himself. Then she sighed. True, she could pretend none of it had ever happened and no one would ever know—except herself, and that was one person too many. It was no good. She couldn't evade the issue and she couldn't hand it over to her parents. It was time for her to stand alone.

She studied her list again. Suddenly she feld cold. Could Miss Mitchell be some sort of spy? That odd exchange of the booklet—did anyone but spies operate like that? The pamphlet must have contained some sort of instructions or information. And the very next day, the woman had somehow managed to take Mrs. Stimson's place!

Nothing hung together, Nan decided. First, the guide searched her luggage and then she warned her to mind her own business. But perhaps the search was just another kind of warning.

The girl shook her head wearily. None of it made any sense. Why in the world would anyone want to kidnap Dr. Yates? And what could she do about it?

The tight, thick feeling in her chest eased a little when she decided that there wasn't anything she could do. Dr. Yates knew about the danger and he did look very capable of handling it. That settled that. She began to tear the list into very small bits, sighing with relief. It wasn't her job after all.

Her hands stilled when the idea struck her. If she watched Miss Mitchell, she might be able to prevent any kidnap attempt. She wished that the thought hadn't occurred to her, but it had. And it was something she could do. She had the distinct impression Miss Mitchell was keeping a close eye on her, too. Perhaps she and the guide could take turns watching each other.

She drew out another sheet of paper and tried to write to her parents. Somehow, she couldn't shed her somber mood—and she wasn't going to send that sort of letter!

A shadow crossed over the desk and Leslie languidly dropped into an easy chair by her side. "What are you doing? You've been among the missing for hours."

"Oh, I'm trying to write my parents and I can't seem to get started."

"Why bother?" Leslie said, her face as sullen as it'd been that first day in New York. "They sort of dumped you overboard, too, didn't they?"

Too surprised to answer for a moment, Nan suddenly understood a number of things—Leslie's stiff welcome in New York, her clouded expression when Nan asked if she weren't having a fabulous time. She *was* having fun, but she didn't want to admit it. For some reason, she thought the trip had been pushed off on her, that her parents wanted to get rid of her.

When Nan finally spoke, her voice was gentle. "Why do you say I was dumped, too?"

"Well, weren't you? That's what it sounded like the day we boarded. If your parents really wanted you around you could've skipped a year of school or they could've stayed home. They didn't *have* to go to Ethiopia."

Nan started to reply, but she remembered her mother's frequent admonition: "Take care what you say. It's so easy to hurt others—and, often as easy to help." So she held back her retort and instead asked softly, "What makes you think your parents don't want you around?"

Leslie shrugged. "Oh, it's pretty clear. And it's even worse than your parents. At least you get to go home next year." She bent her head and clasped her hands tightly together. "My father died four years ago," she continued dully, not looking up. "And last year, Mother met my . . . stepfather. I didn't worry at first, because he wasn't in Washington very often. He's a foreign correspondent. But they wrote each other a lot and last month they got married." She paused, then continued. "We've always lived in Virginia. On a farm. It has white rail fences and a big apple orchard and a stable. Dad and I rode a lot."

The girl was silent again, then her face became rigid and her violet eyes grew cold. "And now she's married this fellow and we'll never live there again. He travels all over Europe and Mother's going with him. They'll have an apartment in Paris, but they won't be there very often. So while they're honeymooning, I'm on this tour. And this fall, I'm supposed to go to a boarding school in Paris."

Nan suggested, "There are lots of ways to look at things. I suppose I could've been very upset when my parents decided to go to Ethiopia. I was looking forward to being a junior in school. Instead, I'm going to be an odd duck in Edinburgh where I don't know a soul. I may not have a real friend all year. I'll admit it scares me, but I didn't let my parents know that.

"I remember the night it was all settled. Dad was so excited. He's a geologist and it's a marvelous challenge for him. He's going to conduct a basic survey in southwestern Ethiopia to see what minerals can be found. It can mean whole new industries and a higher standard of living. And Mother—you can't imagine what the trip means to her. She's been back to Scotland only once since she and Dad were married almost twenty years ago. Because the government pays for their passage to Africa, they'll be able to manage a visit to Scotland on their way home next year. And yet, I don't believe they would have gone if I'd really put up a howl. But they were so eager and happy I couldn't ruin it. They have their lives to lead, too."

"It isn't the same thing at all," Leslie protested. "Mother didn't have to marry Rowley. That's my stepfather, Rowley Latimer. We were very happy until he came along."

"Do you honestly think so?" Nan asked. "Don't you imagine your mother was lonely? And what if she hadn't married him? You'll be going away to college year after next and then she wouldn't have had anyone."

Leslie's face didn't soften, but her eyes flickered uncertainly.

Nan followed her advantage. "And, my friend, consider this—if your mother and stepfather didn't want you around, they certainly wouldn't put you in school in Paris. There are lots and lots of boarding schools in the U.S."

"I'll bet *he'd* like for me to be in the U.S." Leslie stood up abruptly and said, "Come on, helpful one. Let's forget all about parents, schools, and the winter to come. Let's go play."

Nan followed her friend out of the writing room. She hadn't helped Leslie to feel any better. Catching sight of her troubled expression in a gilt-framed mirror, Nan managed a small smile. Her summer had seemed so simple on the surface and now it was swarming with complications—a spy (perhaps), a kidnapping plot (she hoped not), a very upset roommate (that was certain), and, she added last, there was also Jack.

7

A WALK IN MONTMARTRE

Nan's travel alarm sprang to life in the netting next to her bunk. Groping slowly, then more frantically, she pulled it free and pushed in the button. She sank back onto her pillow and almost drifted to sleep again. And then she remembered—this morning the *Constantine* docked at Le Havre . . . next stop, Paris.

Opening her eyes, she peered at the clock's luminous dial. Four o'clock in the morning. Why had she promised to meet Jack to see the sunrise and watch for the first sight of land! But she was already pushing her covers back, wincing from the chill of the cabin. Her cabinmates had better sense than to get up before dawn with only a few hours' sleep.

She stumbled to the bathroom and splashed her face with cold water. It was painful but effective. She felt more like a human being, and excitement began to sparkle in her eyes. On second thought, it was a wonderful way to begin the day.

Hurrying, she slipped into the yellow cotton shirtwaist dress she'd set out the evening before. She stepped into her white flats, pulled on her all-weather coat and picked up her purse.

An eerie quiet blanketed the corridors. She felt like an intrusive ghost, unseen and unheard, her only link with reality the gentle, steady movement of the ship as it steamed on.

She paused for a moment to look up the shadowy length of the main staircase. She'd rushed up and down the stairs so many times in the past five days that they'd become part of a world in which she felt at home. In a way, she'd like to stay on the liner. Dr. Yates was certainly safe enough on it. Once ashore, she had to make good her promise to herself of keeping an eye on Miss Mitchell. Then she shrugged and started swiftly up the steps. She'd worry about that when the time came.

Jack was waiting on the sun deck. Darkness still lay thick and heavy over the ship, but in the east a few streaks of pearl and pale gray were appearing.

Leaning against the railing at the bow, they sipped hot coffee from Jack's thermos and huddled in their coats to watch the slow pulsing of light spread over the sky. It was like riding on top of the world as the sea seemed to curve downward to meet the expanding horizon.

Impulsively, Nan put her hand on the boy's arm. "Thanks for asking me." She glowed as the wind sang in her hair and the tangy scent of the sea enveloped her.

They stayed at the bow long after the clear sunlight turned the stiff whitecaps into glittering, diamond-bright patches. Almost before it seemed possible, Jack hit the rail excitedly with his palm. "There it is—France!"

At first, the land looked like nothing more than a gray bank of clouds low on the horizon. Slowly, it became clearer. Rugged, steep cliffs jutted into the sea.

Fascinated, the girl strained to see everything. But when the ship slowly pulled into the harbor, she turned to her friend, a little disappointed. "The buildings don't look very old—or French."

An amused laugh sounded behind them. "Le Havre's a shock to tourists," Dr. Yates said, joining them. "It's the most modern city in France. Of course, it wasn't planned that way. It was the most heavily bombed port in World War II, so the harbor and city have been almost totally rebuilt. But don't worry, Nan. Paris won't disappoint you."

Four days later, she remembered his words with a laugh as she sat in the hotel writing room, trying to describe the City of Light in a letter to her mother and father. She didn't know where to begin. There was the massive, yet graceful Cathedral of Notre Dame. And the Eiffel Tower. She smiled, remembering the candlelight dinner there with Jack and the lovely tone of the violins. And the Louvre, the world-renowned museum with its almost inexhaustible supply of treasures. She understood better now the magic of the Mona Lisa, with her wise, sad eyes and enigmatic smile. And there was the Champs-Élysées, the broad and elegant boulevard with its trees, sidewalk cafés, and gaiety.

She snapped the cap on her pen. The letter to her parents could wait another day. She couldn't spend her last afternoon in Paris in a hotel lounge! She glanced at her watch. It was almost four o'clock. She was sorry now that she'd refused when Jack invited her to walk along the Seine. Suddenly she got an idea, grabbed her purse and hurried through the old, dimly-lit lobby to the narrow street. She hailed a taxi, which was an extravagance—but hang the expense on her final day in Paris! When the cab neared Montmartre, the old nineteenth century artists' quarter, Nan leaned excitedly against the front seat. There it was—the shimmering, gleaming white dome of Sacre Coeur shining in the sunlight.

The taxi dropped her at the base of broad, terraced limestone steps that lead up to the church crowning the hill of Montmartre. She climbed slowly, stopping often to gaze up at the white basilica.

At the top of the terrace, she turned to see Paris spread below her, the Eiffel Tower in the distance. She sat for a long time—watching the city, while hundreds of tourists—Spanish and Italian, English and American—clambered past. Delighted with the day, she toured the church leisurely, finding the tourists as interesting as Sacre Coeur itself. She wandered out of the basilica into the twisting streets of the Montmartre, pausing once to watch a bearded artist painting yet another version of Paris on a canvas. He wore tan trousers and a purple shirt with a white scarf at his throat. She wondered if he really was from Sioux City or Seattle, even though he tried to look so Parisian.

She turned into a steep street that curved so sharply she couldn't see its end. It was ribbon-thin with rough, uneven cobblestones, bounded by cracked and bumpy sidewalks. The buildings were tan or beige and crowded close together. Some were decorated with grilled balconies while others sported gay flower boxes.

Suddenly, she realized it was growing late. Shadows were lengthening in the old street. And she was hungry.

A small, neat café beckoned across the way. Peering through the window past the menu taped to the glass, she saw several small tables covered with red-and-white checkered tablecloths, a jukebox, and a soda fountain. So much for old France, she thought wryly.

Nan pushed through the wooden swinging doors, sat at a table beside the front window and ordered *café au lait* and an eclair. She finished the eclair in record time, but lingered over her coffee as she watched the sky turn amber as a soft cloak of dusk enveloped the street.

Nan's attention was first caught by the familiarity of the walk. She watched the lone pedestrian almost absently, noting the too-long black dress that seemed indefinably French. But the walk didn't go with the dress. The woman should have moved slowly, deliberately, but that graceful stride, that slender figure—no, it was impossible. Soon she'd be having hallucinations and everywhere she'd see Miss Mitchell in a different garb . . . as an airline hostess, as a nurse, as a chambermaid . . . but Nan didn't really think this was just her imagination.

She set down the thick white cup and peered tensely through the window. The woman was almost directly across the street now. She wore a black scarf wound around her head. Sunglasses, another jarring note with the somber black dress, masked her eyes. But Nan wasn't fooled. She'd been too aware of the woman's every movement for the past few days to be deceived.

It was Miss Mitchell. And she certainly wasn't admiring the beauties of Montmartre in that peculiar costume. She obviously didn't want to be recognized, but where was she going?

Nan hesitated for a moment, then abruptly pushed back her chair. Only she had seen Miss Mitchell. Only she could follow and perhaps learn more of the plot against Dr. Yates.

Hurrying to the cash register, the girl requested, "*L'addition, s'il vous plaît*" in her best high school French, and placed a five-hundred-franc note on the counter.

She waited impatiently while the proprietor slowly counted out her change. Clutching the coins in her hand, she raced for the door. At the curb she gazed to her left. Had she lost Miss Mitchell already? The girl began to run down the sidewalk. She stubbed her toe on a jutting brick and almost crashed into a group of elderly American women. "Well . . . really . . ." and "These youngsters . . ." she heard them sputter in offended tones.

Reaching the spot where the street curved, she put on an

extra bit of speed. For a moment she thought she was too late. Then a black-garbed figure moved out of the shadows at the end of the block and turned into a cross street. As the woman moved out of view, a big, shambling man lumbered out from behind a newspaper kiosk at the corner. He walked quickly despite his clumsy gait and entered the cross street about twenty yards behind the woman.

Nan stared after them. The man wouldn't afford much camouflage, but perhaps she'd be a little less noticeable behind him. She ran to the corner almost on tiptoe and looked around. The street climbed steeply, then cut sharply. The man was nowhere to be seen, but she finally located Miss Mitchell in the darkness of an apartment house stoop. The woman bent near the door. It opened suddenly and she slipped inside.

Nan drew back in surprise against the wall of a butcher shop. The shambling man was emerging from an alley across the street from the apartment house. Hurriedly, he moved to the door which had just closed behind the guide. He fumbled at the lock, but finally it opened and he too disappeared inside.

What did all this mean? Nan wondered. Were Miss Mitchell and the awkward man co-conspirators going to a rendezvous? She remembered the man's stealthy exit from the newspaper kiosk and again from the alleyway. If he wasn't the guide's ally, it meant someone else was following the mysterious Miss Mitchell!

Nan gazed at the building with fright. The old, worn apartment house seemed shrouded in evil. Even the lights shining brightly from the second and fourth floors couldn't dispel the atmosphere of mystery created by Miss Mitchell and her big, awkward follower. As Nan stared, a light came on in a third-floor front window. She waited impatiently. Who was on whose side didn't matter at the moment. She knew only that danger threatened Dr. Yates. Instead of standing next to plate glass decorated with portraits of roasts, pork chops and sausages, she should be trying to find out what Miss Mitchell was up to.

Once she'd decided to follow she moved purposefully up the street to the apartment house, slipped up the steps and turned the doorknob. Locked. She twisted it again. Still locked.

She looked around and her gaze stopped at the alley where the shambling man had hidden. Montmartre must be honeycombed with alleys. She was almost sure there was a gap between the old buildings across the street from the café. It might be an alleyway.

Nan hurried back the way she had come and found the opening midway up the block. The alley was no more than five feet wide, and it turned abruptly after a few feet. An overturned garbage can, a tangle of rotting boards and several broken bottles was all she could see.

Nan knew that her mother would have had an absolute fit if she could have seen her at that moment. A narrow, twisting alley in a strange city with night closing in was no place to be. She held back for a moment, then compromised with her own common sense—she'd leave when night fell absolutely but not before. Taking a deep breath, she went into the debris-filled passageway.

8

A MILLION PIECES . . .

Nan walked slowly into the dim alley, unsure of her footing on the rough cobblestones. She had gone perhaps twenty yards when a rear door swung wide. A man wearing a ragged, once-white apron backed out of the building, carrying two loads of garbage. He turned to dump his burden and stopped short. His eyes widened. Still holding the refuse, he frowned and said, "*Mademoiselle, ce n'est pas un bon endroit pour une jeune fille.*"

He was right. This wasn't a good place for her to be, but, driven by her Scotch stubbornness, she said as she brushed past, "*Merely je vais partir. Merci.*"

She wished she *were* leaving as the passage angled steeply upward and the darkness grew almost impenetrable. This was nothing short of foolhardy. But she had to finish what she had begun.

Suddenly, the loud shriek of a trumpet blared through the alley, resounding among the old walls. She gasped. As the girl drew nearer, she could hear loud talk and the rattle of glassware, but the isolated gaiety made the dark alleyway even more cheerless. She shivered in her light sweater and walked on.

The only illumination came now from lights in the buildings. Night had fallen in Montmartre, but Nan was too engrossed in her adventure to turn back. The girl picked her way ahead carefully. She passed an unshaded window and saw a young mother spooning dinner to a baby in a wooden highchair, its tray shiny from use. The girl felt like an intruder, unseen, unwelcome.

She paused, uncertain. Surely she'd soon be behind the building which Miss Mitchell had entered. She looked at the walls which hemmed her in. Wait! The building had been four floors high, its neighbor only two. This was it, directly ahead and to her left.

Enough light filtered through the shaded windows to disclose a short flight of steps leading to the back entrance of the apartment house. Quietly she mounted the steps and tried the door. It was locked.

Balked but still determined, Nan considered the windows of the first floor. No. She just couldn't climb into someone's apartment. There were limits. Then she saw the pale sheen of windows alongside the pavement. The cellar!

She hurried down the steps and dropped to her hands and knees by the nearest window. She grimaced at the feel of dirt all around her. The whole alley exuded a miasma of decay and grime. But she had come this far, she told herself. She could at least try the cellar windows.

Excitement welled through her when she found the lower sash cracked about an inch. Slipping her fingers beneath it, she pulled. It didn't budge. Not enough leverage. She moved her hands up on the frame and pushed as hard as she could. The sash gave grudgingly. She shoved again and again, wincing as splinters from the rotting wood pricked her palms. Each time the frame squeaked as she pushed, but no sound came from within.

The sash finally stuck, but she had a clear foot of space. Her feet were through the opening and she was beginning to curve like a lopsided S when it occurred to her that she didn't have an inkling what was inside.

Midway through the window, she rolled over on her stomach to get a good grip on the sill. She took a deep breath, bent her knees and let go.

She landed with a jarring thump, but in one piece. She ran a dusty, scratched hand through her hair and savored a small spark of triumph. She was on her way!

She waited a moment for her eyes to adjust to the absolute darkness. But no matter how she strained, the thick blackness remained impenetrable. Slowly she groped along the damp walls and made a circuit of the room.

No stairs. Panic nibbled at her. Moving too quickly, her hands stretched in front of her, she lunged toward the center of the cellar, crashed into an ankle-high obstruction and fell flat, jolting every bone. She pulled herself cautiously to her knees, scraped and bruised, but all parts were in working order. Thrusting out a hand to discover what had thrown her, she patted a step, above it another. Nan grimaced. That was one way to find the stairs.

She limped up the steps and at the top gently turned the knob. The door swung open. She poked her head out gingerly, and saw a small, shabby hallway with peeling painted walls. It was lit by a small naked bulb set in a wall sconce. The odor of cooking fish hovered thickly. A child cried out, "*Maman! Maman!*" but no one appeared in the corridor.

Nan stepped out and drew the cellar door shut behind her. Now to find the guide. She paused. She hadn't really thought beyond gaining access to the building. Then she remembered the light that began to shine from the third story after Miss Mitchell went into the building. Yes, there'd been time for the woman to reach the third floor.

Somewhere in the front of the house a radio played. A man coughed behind a nearby door, but the hall remained empty. On the staircase, Nan hugged the wall to avoid making the old wooden stairs creak. A light burned on the second-floor landing. She glanced around, then started up the steps leading to the next floor—and, she hoped, to Miss Mitchell.

The darkness stopped her. No glimmer of light on the stairs from the third-floor landing. Had the hall light burned out? The back of her neck prickled. Tiptoeing, her throat tight, she reached the top. Very carefully, a breath at a time, she inched her face into the hall. Slowly, her eyes adjusted to the darkness. A faint light gleamed from beneath a door at the front of the hall. The girl's eyes narrowed. The little block of light was interrupted. Suddenly, the darkness was deeper and blacker in front of the door, and she could make out the heavy form of a man pressed next to the jamb.

Nan drew back. The shambling man had found Miss Mitchell too. The hulking black shadow frightened her, and her heart began to race in terror. She could feel the staircase vibrating as someone climbed slowly, step by heavy step. No one who lived in an apartment house would come home that way. This was another silent figure of the night.

She was trapped! Ahead—the shambling man. Below—the furtive climber.

She was suddenly grateful for the dark landing. She dropped to her stomach on the floor of the hall, and as quietly as a fish gliding through water, crawled in the black shadow to the steps leading up to the fourth floor. She made it just in time. Lying on the treads, she peered through the banister to watch the arrival of the climber.

The black hulk by the apartment door started, then slipped across the hall to melt into another pool of darkness. He'd been alerted by some vagrant noise. She wondered if it'd been made by her or by the nameless climber on the stairs.

The climber carefully surveyed the apparently empty hall, then moved to the door with its telltale line of light. He knocked—tap, tap, tap, tap—and the door opened. Wearing coveralls and a railroad cap, the man slipped inside. The door shut behind him, but not before the girl glimpsed the woman in a too-long black dress.

In an instant the shambling man crossed the hall to resume his post.

Nan decided she must find out what was happening in that apartment. She began to inch her way up the stairs. Once out of sight from the landing, she rose and tiptoed to the top floor. She could hear muted voices in the apartment across the stairs. She walked quickly up the hall until she was above the apartment where Miss Mitchell had welcomed the man in the railroad cap. The dim bulb above the fourth-floor landing gave enough light to show there were no convenient gratings which might let her hear their conversation. The girl looked up and down the corridor. Her gaze fastened on the door at the end of the hall. It would lead to the slender balcony which ran the width of the building on each floor.

She walked unwillingly to the door. Despite their iron grillwork, the balconies had looked so insubstantial in the soft light of dusk, as if they were meant for decoration rather than use. But there wouldn't be a door to the balcony if it were unsafe.

She grasped the door's brass handle, squeezing it so tightly that its ridges hurt her fingers. It was not the safety of the balcony that concerned her. It was its distance from the ground.

"Listen, Nan," she told herself quietly, "Somebody's trying to kidnap Dr. Yates. And you're the only one who can do anything to stop it. You've got to."

As she opened the door, she remembered the day her tree house collapsed and the breathless, tumbling instant that seemed to stretch into an eternity as she fell through the air.

This wasn't a tree house—it was a balcony. And it was night. She wouldn't be able to see down. All she had to do was pretend she was on a little porch. Anybody could walk out on a porch. But porches aren't four stories high—an unhappy thought.

She slipped through the doorway onto the balcony—and felt it quiver with her weight. She crouched to clutch the foot-high railing that was the only barrier between her and the pavement four stories below. When the pounding of her heart slowed, she edged beneath lighted windows until she was directly above the apartment where Miss Mitchell had greeted the man in the railroad cap.

On her hands and knees, Nan carefully leaned over the short railing, determinedly ignoring the uncertain movement of the balcony and the long distance to the street.

Soft voices came to her faintly.

"He knows who I am."

"And he still doesn't take it seriously?" a man's voice asked.

"No." The cool, blunt reply was in Miss Mitchell's unruffled voice.

Nan's eyes widened. She leaned farther over the railing.

The man gave a short, bitter laugh. "He has no judgment. But your cover isn't spoiled as long as he keeps quiet."

"I think he will," she answered calmly.

"Good. Your instructions are to keep a careful watch so that we'll be prepared when the time is ripe." The girl heard the shuffle of paper. "I haven't been told for sure, but the likeliest site for the kidnapping is Trieste, the international port between Italy and Yugoslavia. We expect you to . . ."

And then the night split into a million pieces!

9

NO LONGER ALONE

"Gendarme! Gendarme!" the woman screamed shrilly. *"Voilà un voleur. Au secours! Vite. Vite. Gendarme!"*

The high, frightened shriek struck against Nan with an almost physical force. In a daze, she turned around. Only an arm's length away, a frowsy blonde in an unkempt bathrobe leaned out of the fourth-floor window to point at the balcony—and her. The woman thought she was a thief! Nan watched in awful fascination as her accuser's stubby hand stabbed the air.

A chair crashed to the floor in the apartment below her. The guide and the man! They mustn't see her. The fear which had held her in a frozen trance turned to flame. Awkwardly but quickly she scooted backward toward the door opening onto the hall. She had no more than stumbled through it than the blonde's apartment door swung open. The woman's shrill cries filled the hall.

Nan ran headlong down the hall and clattered down the steps. The third-floor landing was still dark, but a thin wedge of light shone from the cracked door of the front apartment. But it was too dark for the guide and man to see her.

As she raced on down the stairs, Nan could hear voices calling out. And then she heard the heavy thud of footsteps close behind. The shambling man was chasing her!

On the ground floor, she started for the front door then swerved and turned for the back as a front apartment opened. She pounded down the hall and in the dim light of the wall sconce, frantically loosened the bolt to the back door.

Plunging through the door, she slammed it behind her and half-fell, half-ran down the steps into the alley. Though her ankle twinged painfully, she noticed it only slightly. The door was opening behind her as she began to run down the passageway.

Windows were flung open. Other voices called through the night.

"Gendarme! Gendarme!"

The girl ran on, thankful for her soft-soled shoes, even though the rough cobblestones hurt her feet. But she had to find cover! At any moment the police would come.

Over the shouting voices, she heard someone running behind her. Rounding one of the alleyway's abrupt little turns, she looked desperately about. Behind those garbage cans? Her pace didn't slacken. No good. She must get inside one of the buildings. Her pursuer was drawing closer.

Garbage cans! That man who'd warned her! Perhaps he'd help. She forced an even faster gait and rounded another of the passage's turns—it'd been just about here. A sob of relief tore at her throat. There—where the row of cans stood two deep. She threw herself at the door, pulled it open and stumbled inside.

Breathing harshly, she leaned against the wall in the dingy little hall, her face and hands pressed hard against the grainy points of the stippled plaster. She could smell the sharp tang of onions and garlic and the rich fullness of braising meat. Pans rattled and footsteps tapped hurriedly somewhere to the left of the hall. The odors and bustling noises were reassuring. Danger and cooking don't go hand in hand—then someone ran lumberingly around the turn in the alley. She pushed closer to the wall like a hunted animal.

The steady pounding against the pavement beat into her until, scarcely breathing, she realized it was past. Her pursuer hadn't caught her.

The girl's fingers relaxed their pressure against the sharp-grained plaster.

Suddenly, a man's voice in the nearby kitchen broke into a torrent of angry French. A nervous, obsequious voice replied, "*Oui, oui, a l'instant même. Je me dépêche.*"

With a clatter and a stumble, the kitchen worker who had warned her earlier in the evening backed into the hall, carrying three garbage cans. Still talking to his tormentor, he turned and saw Nan. The girl bent forward imploringly. "*S'il vous plaît, j'ai besoin de me cacher. Aidez-moi, s'il vous plaît.*"

The man peered over his shoulder nervously, then looked again into Nan's dark, desperate eyes. As someone began to storm angrily toward the hall door, a mischievous smile flickered across the worker's face, and he said loudly, "*Non, mademoiselle, le lavabo n'est pas par ici. C'est à gauche. Oui, de rien.*" He turned to face the kitchen, his garbage cans blocking her from view as she slipped past. As she hurried up the narrow hall, she could hear him explaining, "It's nothing. A young woman who lost her way to the ladies' room. Yes, yes, I'm hurrying. . . ."

Nan blessed the little man who'd helped her as she pushed through a velvet curtain over the exit at the end of the hall. He'd given her a chance to get free from the nightmare that had swallowed her when the frowsy blonde woman began to scream. The girl moved hesitantly in the dim light of a musty room stacked with unused tables and chairs, but she quickened her steps when she saw the ladies' room. Ducking into the restroom, she felt a sharp qualm as an old woman rose to offer her a towel. In the dim light, the crone's eyes slid incuriously over her, missing her soiled clothes and smudged face. Or perhaps, Nan thought as she scrubbed her hands, the old attendant no longer saw people as individuals, but only as tips, a means to life.

Taking her time, the girl tried to make herself presentable after the fumbling journey through the cellar and her ragged flight down the alley. Finally there was no more dust to be brushed from her dress, her hair was neat, her face and hands clean. She could pass muster in a dim light—and she couldn't wait any longer. She had to find a way out of the restaurant. She paused at the door, then resolutely opened it. A murmur of voices and the soft cry of violins flowed from the dining room.

How could she possibly walk through the restaurant? Past all those waiters and the *maitre d' hotel* and perhaps even a doorman? But she couldn't stand there all night either.

Throwing her head back, she walked briskly into the dining room and threaded her way among the tables. She passed waiters carrying trays and others wheeling carts, but she didn't look at them. She neared the entrance and the *maître d'hôtel.* With a smile, Nan nodded to him. "*Bon soir*," she said pleasantly, "we enjoyed our dinner very much." A puzzled look flashed briefly over his dark face, but he inclined his head and murmured, "*Bon soir, mademoiselle*." He paused and inquired very delicately, "Your escort. . . ?"

"He's getting the car. Thank you again for such a nice evening." The headwaiter bowed a second time as she walked through the front door.

She'd done it—if no one came charging after her. Halfway

up the block, she flagged a cruising cab, and sank into the sagging back seat. *"L'hôtel Victoria Palace, s'il vous plaît. Six Rue Blaise-Desgoffes."*

The girl sat limply as the taxi bounced across Paris. She was still in a tired daze when she paid the driver and walked slowly into the hotel. She skirted past the lounge where she heard some of the tour members singing, "It's a Long, Long Way to Tipperary." Where, she wondered irrelevantly, was Tipperary?

The elevator rumbled slowly up, and when it stopped on her floor, she pushed herself away from the back wall with an effort. Only a few more feet and she'd be in her room. She'd take a hot bath, but she wouldn't think, not now, not tonight.

The pleasant thought carried her all the way down the hall, but when she opened the door and saw Leslie and Jack, she knew it was just a fantasy.

It was the first time she had seen Jack without a smile.

"Where in the world have you been?" Leslie began, her voice edgy with worry.

Jack broke in, his face grim. "What happened?"

As Nan stepped into the room and closed the door behind her, she saw his eyes widen as he glimpsed her scratched hands and dirt-smudged dress.

"Are you all right?" he asked.

"Please!" she pleaded. "I'm so tired!"

Leslie hurried to her side and pulled her toward the couch. "Sit down," she urged. "Take your time, but you must tell us what's wrong. We'll help."

The exhausted girl leaned back in the uncomfortable horsehair sofa and rubbed her eyes wearily. She just wanted to forget everything and take a hot bath and go to bed—but none of those things would make the image of Miss Mitchell go away. She lifted her eyes and looked at Jack and Leslie. They were waiting—and they wanted to help. She broke into a smile. There was no reason in the world she shouldn't let them. After all, she hadn't told her parents because they were so far away and so helpless. But here, in front of her, were two friends who would do the best they could. She didn't have to be alone any longer.

She sat up on the edge of the cushion. "You're right, Leslie. I need help. I've stumbled onto something very—ugly. And I don't know what to do about it."

She told them everything, right from the beginning—the museum, Mrs. Stimson, the conversation between Dr. Yates and Miss Mitchell, the guide's warning, the meeting in Montmartre, the shambling man.

The boy and girl listened in absolute stillness. When she finished, Jack said, "Whew! I'll say you got mixed up in something. But why didn't you tell me sooner?"

"I was afraid you might think I was sort of hysterical," she said quietly. "It was all so nebulous—until tonight." She sank back on the couch, relaxed and at ease. She had help now.

"I'd never have thought that," said Jack.

"Okay, kids," Leslie interrupted, "we can have the balcony scene another time. Right now, we need to think."

They studied it from every angle. Jack suggested taking her information to the American Embassy in Paris.

"But we leave here in the morning," Leslie objected. "What could they do?"

"And the Paris police couldn't help," Nan said. "After all, if a crime is being plotted, it isn't planned for Paris."

"They could contact the police authorities in Trieste," Leslie suggested.

Jack suddenly pounded his fist against the arm of his chair. "We're idiots!" he shouted. "The thing to do is obvious."

The girls stared at him in surprise.

"All we have to do," he said, "is tell Dr. Yates everything that Nan's learned. And he can take it from there."

If only he would, Nan thought, if only he would. How nice it would be to turn it all over to the professor. But when she remembered Dr. Yates' insistence that no one was going to kidnap him, she wondered how much he would welcome any more talk about the plot.

"I don't know," she began doubtfully.

"Jack's right," Leslie insisted.

Nan gave in finally, but she refused to confront the professor alone.

"We'll all go," Leslie suggested, her violet eyes flashing with excitement.

"It would be better—" Jack started to say.

Nan straightened up stiffly. "Jack O'Neill, I won't do it. I won't, I tell you."

"Don't break the sound barrier," he ordered in disgust. "If that isn't just like a girl! All right, I'll go with you. Let's go before I change my mind. Girls!"

She smiled at him, because his gray eyes were warm and kind. "Boys!" she rejoined. "Always bossing people around."

"I'd love to go," Leslie said, "but it would be too much like a delegation. But hurry back and give me the scoop."

Nan and Jack went down the shadowed hall and stopped in front of Dr. Yates' room. A light shone under his door.

Jack patted her on the shoulder, then knocked on the panel. A chair was pushed back and the door swung open. Holding a book in one hand and his pipe in the other, Dr. Yates looked surprised, but he smiled. "Good evening. Come in."

He waved them to a seat on a horsehair sofa, the twin of the one in the girls' room.

Jack spoke first. "Sir, Nan has stumbled onto an—odd situation and she wants to tell you about it."

The older man closed his book and looked at the girl searchingly. "What's the problem?" he asked.

She began in a rush. "It's about Miss Mitchell." She paused when his face changed into a grim mask. "You see," she continued, "I happened to overhear your conversation with her on the ship—about someone wanting to kidnap you." The professor started to interrupt, but Nan hurried on. "But that's not what I came to tell you. Tonight I saw her in Montmartre."

Dr. Yates cut in abruptly, his voice strangely sardonic. "Probably she was wearing a disguise, which didn't fit, perhaps a trench coat, and she went off to a secret rendezvous with some other sinister figure dressed the same way."

Nan gazed at him steadily. "You seem to think it's all very funny, sir, but what I heard tonight wasn't the least bit funny."

The big man tightened his jaws, flushed, and replied angrily, "Perhaps it isn't a joke. That doesn't mean it isn't ridiculous." He stopped for a moment, then continued in a softer voice. "I know about Miss Mitchell. And she doesn't worry me, she annoys me. I can take care of myself, and I don't need anyone's help."

Nan stood up and said, "I'm very sorry if I've annoyed you—"

Jack cut in harshly. "Look here, Dr. Yates, Nan's gone through quite a bit tonight."

The girl caught his arm. "Let's forget it. Dr. Yates doesn't want our help."

The professor caught her at the door. "I'm sorry, I didn't mean what I just said. I'm sorry, too, that you've been mixed up in this piece of make-believe. I only meant that I know what's going on and it's obviously ridiculous. Now you two forget that you ever heard anything about it and enjoy your trip. Okay?"

Nan tried one more time as she stood in the doorway. "Dr. Yates, what I saw wasn't make-believe, it was—"

His face tightened. "No. I meant what I said. Forget it. Good night."

And they were in the hall, staring at his closed door.

Back in the girls' room, Jack was all for washing their hands of it.

"That guy doesn't want our help. Let him get kidnapped," he fumed. "It'd serve him right."

He was angry because the professor had refused to listen to Nan. Although the realization touched her, she urged, "Don't be irritated. Dr. Yates isn't at all stupid, you know, so he must have a reason for brushing us off." Nan paused thoughtfully. "Let's pin it down. He's convinced that this kidnapping threat is ridiculous. But at the same time, I know that Miss Mitchell and the man in the railroad cap were serious." She looked at her friends. "You do believe that, don't you?"

"Of course we do," Leslie replied without hesitation. "But the whole thing's so strange!"

"It can only mean," Jack said, "that Dr. Yates is wrong, because both he and Nan can't be right, and I'll put my faith in Nan."

"So where does that leave us?" Leslie demanded wearily.

Nan's dark eyes were somber and worried when she answered, "It leaves us as the only ones who know that Dr. Yates is really in danger."

10

LETTER FROM MR. LATIMER

Once they'd left Paris and were riding along in the small bus that would transport them over Europe, all the puzzling events seemed a little unreal and not half so frightening. The soft green beauty of the Loire Valley, with its gentle slopes and stately poplars, made kidnappings planned in dingy rooms seem improbable—something to be read about, not lived.

The magnificent castles of the Loire, dominating the land as in the past they had dominated the lives of the neighboring villages, captured the travelers' imaginations.

"They're fantastic," Nan said to Leslie as the students clambered back on the bus after viewing their third chateau of the day. "But frankly, they don't look like castles. They're so—well, so dignified!" And she sounded a little plaintive.

Nan slipped into her seat right behind Dr. Yates. Although he should certainly be safe enough on the bus, the watchdog committee, as Jack had dubbed them, was taking no chances.

Nan's blonde roommate plumped down next to her and

replied, "I know. I suppose we got our ideas of castles from *Lorna Doone* and *Ivanhoe.* We should have expected the French to be graceful in all things—even castle-building."

The coach door closed and the bus began to chug away on its way to Tours. The late afternoon sun bathed the gently rolling countryside with a soft, translucent light. The huge castles didn't look as though people had lived colorful and violent lives in them. They were symmetrical and staid. But behind their ornate facades, battles had been planned and men's lives balanced in the hands of kings. And, often enough, those in favor one day found themselves the next day imprisoned deep within Amboise, a white chateau with dignity and charm—and cells for prisoners of state.

But the reality of intrigue and danger faded as the days tumbled over one another. The bus traveled southeast across France, leaving the gentle lowlands to wind through the rugged, volcanic plateau country of central France, then to thread breathtakingly through the Alps, where snowcapped mountains thrust their peaks boldly into the sky.

Each day, Nan grew more relaxed. The beauty of the towering mountains made Paris, with its roaring traffic and centuries-old streets, seem long ago and far away.

The letter came in Avignon.

They arrived about six o'clock Monday evening, weary after a long day on the bus. The usual routine began. Milling around in the lobby of the small hotel, the students waited for Miss Mitchell to hand out room keys and for the driver to unload their luggage. Nan looked for the desk clerk. Usually he was on hand immediately with the mail. She was hoping that tonight there would be a letter for her. Her parents should have had a chance to write by now. The gaunt lady who managed the hotel hovered near Miss Mitchell, saying in a high, thin voice, "The bus is late. We have dinner awaiting your group in the dining room."

Nan scanned the lobby again. Ornately carved stairs, their carpet worn in the center, curved out of sight. Velvet curtains framed the dining room, where she could see a long table set for dinner. Nearby, a waiter listlessly waved flies away from a serving table. A young man, his long hair swept back on either side, snapped something to the busboy and strode into the lounge. He wore a dark suit and a self-important expression. It had to be the desk clerk.

Then Leslie rushed up, holding a key triumphantly in the air. "I have it. Let's hurry and freshen up before dinner."

Nan had sighted a lump of mail tucked on the corner of the desk. "Go on without me," she urged. "I think I see our mail."

Leslie shrugged. "None of it will be for me, and yours can keep until after dinner. But stay if you like. See you in a minute." She hurried for the stairs.

Feeling sticky and rumpled, Nan almost followed her, but she stayed behind when she saw the clerk lift the packet and open it. He began to call out names, stumbling over the foreign pronunciation. She listened intently, shot up her hand when Leslie's name was called, and waited to hear her own. Finally all the mail was gone and she held only a letter for her friend. She sighed, dropped it in her purse, and trudged in to dinner.

Leslie was late, and the only seat left was up the table on the side opposite Nan. Nan waved the letter. "You're in luck tonight."

"For me?" Leslie asked, then her face dropped. "Keep it. I'll look at it later."

Nan shook her head slowly at the girl, but Leslie turned defiantly to Annette, a girl who not only dressed like a *Vogue* model, but also insisted on talking about clothes all the time.

It served Leslie right for pouting, Nan thought. Now she'd

have to talk about sweaters and skirts and necklines and hemlines for a whole hour.

In their room after dinner, Nan fished the letter out again. "Come on, friend, someone went to the trouble of writing you. You can read it. And besides, I don't intend to carry it around until it wilts."

Leslie's violet eyes darkened. "Trouble. That's the right word."

"Oh, Leslie," her friend sighed. "Don't be so stubborn."

Grudgingly, Leslie reached for the envelope, but when she saw the handwriting, she started to tear it in half.

For once Nan's gentle voice cracked like a whip. "Stop that!"

Their eyes locked for a long moment. Leslie's dropped first. "All right," she said, "I'll admit I'm half-wrong. I'll at least read it."

She slit the envelope open carelessly and drew out two thin sheets, filled with single-spaced typing. As she read, her face changed and she gave an excited cry.

Full of curiosity, but not daring to say anything, Nan drew water into the small basin and began to wash out two skirts.

"It's from Rowley," Leslie announced. "You know, my stepfather. He's been making a check of his wire service bureaus and one of the reporters in Berlin told him about a tip from a secret agent in Yugoslavia." She paused for emphasis. "This man told the reporter that Yugoslavian agents are planning to kidnap Dr. Yates."

"Yugoslavian agents!" Nan repeated. "So that's why it's supposed to happen in Trieste."

"Right," Leslie said. "Trieste is between Italy and Yugoslavia. Anyway, my stepfather says the minute he heard it was the leader of our tour, he decided to write me." Leslie was pleased, and she continued almost shyly. "This is what he wrote."

"'My dear Leslie, I know that you're not happy about your mother's marriage and in fact are dead set against me. But I'm sure we can work this out in time, because we both love your mother very much and that gives us a great deal in common. However, I'm not writing you tonight about our personal problems, but because you're a level-headed, intelligent girl and I know I can count on you to be discreet and, possibly, very helpful to someone who may need your help.'"

She paused and said, "He said that about me!"

Nan nodded impatiently. "That's wonderful, but what more does he say about Dr. Yates?"

"Oh, Dr. Yates," Leslie said, "that's about all Rowley said about him. Nobody seems to have any idea why Yugoslavia should want to kidnap him. He wants me to keep an eye on the professor and report anything that appears off-key. So the thing for us to do is write and tell Rowley everything you've learned. He'll know what to do—and we can relax and enjoy the Riviera."

The girls composed the letter to Mr. Latimer with care, and when it was finished and given to the desk clerk to mail, Nan felt free and secure for the first time since she'd heard the heavy thud of a man's footsteps nearing the Egyptian chamber in the Metropolitan Museum of Art in New York.

As she lay in her bed that night listening to Leslie's quiet, even breathing, she smiled, thinking of the carefree hours that lay ahead. They'd keep their eyes open, but after all, they didn't need to worry any longer. Mr. Latimer would take care of it.

The next morning Jack swung into the bus and settled in the back with them.

"Hey, girls, I thought we agreed you two would sit close to the prof while I kept a lookout at night." Quietly, they explained everything to him. His dark frown surprised them both.

"You know," Jack said musingly, "maybe Dr. Yates is right. There's something crazy about the whole setup."

Leslie sat up straight in her seat. "What do you mean?" she demanded. "My stepfather doesn't get things wrong."

Her roommate smiled at the new tone in Leslie's voice. It was wonderful what a little trust could do.

"Speak softly," Jack cautioned. "Don't tell the whole bus. I don't mean your stepfather is wrong. I mean this Yugoslavian angle is wrong."

"Why?" Nan asked. "It's a Communist country and, for all we know, Dr. Yates is an expert in something that'd be useful to them."

"So they kidnap him," Jack chided, "and create an international incident with the American government protesting and the newspapers having a field day."

"Why not?" Leslie inquired. "I mean, they're Communists, so why do they care?"

Jack shook his head. "I can tell that you two skipped current events entirely and planned slumber parties in your European history classes. Saying simply that Yugoslavia is a Communist country misses the point," Jack explained.

"Well, just what is the point?" Leslie's tone was sarcastic.

"Although it's Communist," Jack went on, "it's no vassal of the U.S.S.R.—and it's in our interest that it doesn't become one. The United States gives it a lot of aid, although there are many Congressmen and Senators who fight against it bitterly—because it *is* a Communist country. Now do you see why it doesn't make sense? If an American were kidnapped by Yugoslavia, it could hurt our relations with them. And without U.S. aid, Yugoslavia could slide under Russian influence. Tito's been fighting that for years."

Nan's face was puzzled. "You're right. It doesn't make sense—unless Dr. Yates is terribly important in some way."

"I don't think any one person could be that important to them."

"Okay," Leslie said. "We all agree—it doesn't make sense, but it's happening. Now look, let's relax. We've done our part. We'll let Rowley figure it out while we play on the beach at Nice. Agreed?"

"Agreed," Nan replied quickly.

"I'm with you," the boy said. "It's too much for me."

And so while the bus rolled along the trio played Twenty Questions. But when the road reached the coast, they fell silent. Stark, rocky headlands jutted into the vivid blue of the Mediterranean. In the clear, bright light everything sparkled with luxuriant color, the pomegranates orange-red, the evergreens a deep hue, the mimosa-mantled hillsides radiantly golden. The balmy, sea-scented air held a promise of ease and delight.

Next stop: Nice.

11

ONE NIGHT IN NICE

After a late, lazy breakfast of *croissants* with strawberry-jam and coffee, Nan and Leslie set out to explore Nice. They reached the Old Town, where the city had first been built. Pale pink climbing geraniums and purple bougainvillaea carpeted the walls of the pastel villas.

"I don't suppose there's more color anywhere in the world," Nan began when Leslie caught her arm to point up the street.

Thousands of blooms in every shade imaginable flaunted their beauty in wagons, stalls, baskets and carts. The wanderers had discovered Nice's famous Flower Market. Entranced, they went close to admire magenta geraniums, striped carnations, and dark-red dahlias. Leslie came to a full stop beside a wagon-load of delicately scented cream roses. She nodded emphatically to herself and bought an armful.

Leslie carefully shielded the roses from the bustling crowds as they walked down the steep and twisting streets to the new town and the broad Promenade des Anglais, the boulevard which follows the sweeping curve of the Bay of Angels.

Nan made no comment until they'd settled at an outdoor café on the Promenade. She watched with a mischievous grin while Leslie searched for a spot to park her roses. The table was too small. They might be crushed underfoot on the ground. Finally she shrugged, balanced the huge bouquet in her lap, and reached awkwardly over it for her drink.

"Do you plan to hold them all night?" Nan was amused. "Or shall we take turns? I know, we can string them around the room."

Her friend glowered at her. "All right, I'm an idiot. But they were too lovely not to have, and I certainly won't throw them away—even if I do have to hold them all night." She looked away, ignoring Nan, but suddenly a wide smile crossed her face. "I'm not the only one," she cried. "Look!" She began to wave and call, "Miss Dawes! Miss Dawes!"

For a moment the alert face of their cabinmate aboard ship didn't change expression, but then she smiled and crossed the sidewalk to their table. The crimson anemones she carried in her arms blazed with color against her sensible green-and-white striped seersucker suit.

Gesturing with the flowers, she said, "I see that you succumbed, too, Leslie."

Nan laughed and threw up her hands in defeat. "Now I wish I'd bought some, too. Won't you sit down and join us, Miss Dawes?"

The older woman drew up a chair and announced, "This is quite a coincidence. I saw Mrs. Royston earlier this morning."

"How fantastic!" Leslie exclaimed.

"Oh well, it isn't too surprising," Miss Dawes answered. "Few Americans can pass up Nice."

The conversation was relaxed and casual. It centered around Miss Dawes' search for antiques—a combination of business and pleasure, for she owned an antique shop in Rochester, New York.

"But that's not really a good excuse to be here," she said ruefully. "I can't resist a stopover in Nice on every trip, although it hasn't much in my line compared with the rest of France."

The collector discussed her favorite cities in Europe. Nan listened while sipping her limeade and watching the people on the Promenade. A group of German boys in short leather pants tramped by. A French family with a picnic basket, a bottle of wine and a baby decided the beach was perfect just there. Four American girls equipped with movie cameras checked their light meters, then filmed an old, wrinkled man playing an accordion while his monkey mechanically waved a battered cup in the clear, bright air.

Nan's gaze froze. It couldn't be! She craned her head for a better look, but the man was lumbering out of sight now, his awkward gait purposeful and hurried compared to the slow-moving crowd about him.

She jumped up. "Miss Dawes, I'm terribly sorry, but I must go. I see—I see an old friend. Please, Les, get the check and I'll pay you later." And she was off.

Threading her way at a half-run through the milling throng of sightseers, she knew she was terribly noticeable. People didn't race down the Promenade in Nice. They strolled, they sauntered and they meandered, but they didn't run. Startled pigeons fluttered skyward as she raced past. She bumped into the end of a flower cart. Apologizing over her shoulder, she heard the man mutter, "Crazy Americans." But still she ran, scanning the moving mass of people for the shambling man. She couldn't miss him with those heavy shoulders and that awkward walk.

But finally, winded and hot, she stopped and leaned against the tufted bark of a palm tree in despair. She saw American sailors on shore leave, flaxen-haired children from some northern country, proper French families, vacationing students of all sorts. But nowhere in that throng of people could she spot the shambling man. And where, she wondered, was Dr. Yates? It was time for the watchdog committee to swing back into action—if only she could locate the professor.

"The next time we stake out Dr. Yates in bright sunlight on a beach," Leslie said irritably that evening as she spread cold cream on her nose and cheeks, "you can keep watch while I hide under an umbrella, my friend."

"Oh, Les, I'm sorry, but after you left Miss Dawes and joined me and we finally found the professor, I was afraid to leave him."

The blonde girl peered into the dresser mirror, surveyed her sunburnt face critically and added another swipe of the thick white cream. "If I wriggle my nose," she continued in disgust, "I look like a rabbit." Then she shrugged and turned to study her roommate. "Do you really think seeing the shambling man means Dr. Yates is in danger now?"

Nan nodded. "I think the shambling man must be working with Miss Mitchell and the kidnapping is planned for here instead of Trieste."

"But he was listening ouside the door in Montmartre," Leslie objected.

Nan shrugged. "Agents don't trust anybody. They watch each other."

"Are you sure it was really the same man?" Leslie persisted.

"Positive."

"He certainly didn't show up on the beach," the blonde girl said.

"No, but we had to watch Dr. Yates just in case. I think the real danger will be tonight." Nan glanced down at her watch. "I have a plan. I'll tell you about it at dinner, but let's hurry downstairs now and take over watching the professor so Jack will have time to change before dinner."

The girls found Jack at a writing table in an alcove off the main lobby. He had a clear view of the bar and Dr. Yates. The girls stopped short when they saw the professor. He was sharing his small table with Miss Mitchell, and they were laughing together.

"You know," Leslie mused, "I wonder if he deserves protection. Nothing like playing fly to the spider."

Jack grinned. "A very pretty spider," he said. "I wouldn't mind it myself."

"Get out of here before I drape that flowerpot over your head," Nan snapped. "If you think this is funny—"

"Mildly," he insisted teasingly. "Okay, simmer down and watch the man. For some reason or other, we're going to save him from an unknown fate."

The ruggedly built professor and the slender guide were standing now. Miss Mitchell smiled and slowly they walked out of the bar to the dining room. "I'll go on upstairs," Jack said. "Get a table for three and keep tabs on our friend."

Nan picked out a table in a quiet corner where they'd have a clear view of the professor. "This is perfect," she decided. "We won't miss a thing, but we can talk privately."

When Jack hurried in, his hair still damp from a shower, Leslie said to Nan, "Now let's have your plan."

"It's simple," Nan began. "Dr. Yates will either be lured out of his room or someone will get in on one pretext or another and he'll be kidnapped. The snag is this—we don't know what approach they'll use. Someone could call on the telephone or knock on his door—"

"Or shinny up his balcony," Leslie suggested.

"Where's his room?" the boy asked.

"Three balconies down from ours," Nan reported. "We're next to the corner of the hotel. That puts him about in the middle."

"So we have to watch all approaches," Jack said.

"And here's how we'll do it. . . ." Nan whispered.

The night breeze was mild, but Nan shivered and drew her sweater a little closer round her. She sat in the deep shadows of their balcony. The girl had been there for hours, watching while lights blinked out, one by one. Only scattered windows still glowed. The night was overcast and sultry. She didn't really need a sweater, but there was something very chilling about waiting so quietly for the approach of danger. She tried to find Jack in the dense dark of the hotel garden below her. Was he in the black shadow of that big eucalyptus tree or hidden by the trailing branches of the weeping willow near the gate to the street? She knew Leslie was tucked behind the velvet curtains of an alcove in the hall across from Dr. Yates' room.

Would anyone come? And if they should, from which direction?

Clouds drifted across the moon. Its glow lit the sky and gleamed brightly on the empty white garden until another wisp of cloud shrouded its face. In the thick darkness, she could hear the sounds of the night. Leaves rustled softly on the magnolia tree directly beneath her balcony and palm fronds rattled like paper bags. When a nightingale began to sing, his voice clear and perfect, the girl closed her eyes and listened. It was as if all the love and beauty in the world were bound into his song.

In the silence following the nightingale's call, a scraping noise jolted her back to reality. She peered through an opening between the balcony's concrete balustrades. The garden below lay dark and quiet. Nothing moved but the restless branches of the trees.

She strained to hear. And then it came again—a scuffing sound. The clouds parted and the light of the moon suddenly swept over the grounds. Graveled walks gleamed like chalk. Palms swayed gracefully, silhouetted against the sky. But no one crept through the garden.

She turned and very carefully raised her head above the edge of the balcony, her eyes studying the facade of the building. Something moved on the balcony just past Dr. Yates' window. Another cloud slid over the face of the moon. It could be just a potted palm, restless in the breeze. Then a shadow detached itself from the dim overhang of thick vines and moved quietly to the low wall of the balcony. She recognized the scuffing sound—a soft-soled shoe grating on the concrete. The moving shadow stepped noiselessly up on the railing and crouched to jump.

This was it! The intruder had fooled them all. Unaware, Leslie waited in the hall. Jack stood guard in the garden, waiting for a twig to snap. Here was the threat, and only she realized it. The girl stood and clutched the prickly creeper covering the balcony. The shadow jumped, landing with a thump on the professor's balcony.

Nan looked desperately around and then she remembered the night in Montmartre. She began to scream as loud as she could. "Help! Help! A burglar! Help!"

The shadow froze for an instant. Then it whipped around, swung over the edge of the balcony and dropped to the soft ground below. Nan continued to scream. Voices began to call out, in French and English, Italian and German. Lights flashed on. Robed figures appeared on balconies. Leslie ran out crying, "What's happened?"

Nan pointed down, and they leaned over the edge of the railing and watched the fugitive running through the garden toward the gate. A figure launched himself in a flying tackle from behind the eucalyptus tree. It was Jack. The adversaries crashed to the ground. Rolling around, they rattled the gravel on the walk. Nan called out in fear, "Jack! Jack!" as his opponent thrust the boy away, struggled upright and landed a hard kick. Jack slumped onto the ground and the man, running hard, reached the gate, pushed it open and was gone.

Nan whirled over the edge of her balcony, noting only slightly that the thorny creeper was cutting her hands, and dropped the short distance to the ground. She rushed across the garden. Jack was on his hands and knees, shaking his head slowly from side to side. Leslie skidded to a stop beside them.

Nan dropped to his side. "Are you hurt badly?"

"No—I—it stunned me." He tried to scramble to his feet. "Where is he?"

"He got away," Nan said quickly. "Through the gate in the wall."

"And he must have had an accomplice," Leslie added. "I heard a car roar off just after he slipped out."

Jack stood up and leaned unsteadily against the back of a garden seat. "I wasn't much good," he said disgustedly. Then he frowned. "Through the gate? He couldn't have. I checked earlier and it was locked."

"It isn't locked now," Nan said quietly.

The trio tensed as overhead lights flashed on, illuminating the garden. The hotel manager with several bellboys and guests, including Dr. Yates, poured out the side door, prodded by an excited middle-aged man who was exclaiming, "I tell you, there was a battle in the garden and—" The group paused when it saw the boy and two girls, then hurried to them.

His face dark with worry, the manager demanded, "What has happened? What takes place?"

"It must have been a cat burglar," a cool voice answered, and Miss Mitchell stepped forward casually.

"I think it's very clear," the young woman continued. "When the girl began to scream, I ran to my balcony and saw the man. He was startled and jumped into the garden. This boy tried to stop him, but the man was stronger. I ran downstairs and followed him outside, but he climbed into a waiting car and got away. I found this right outside the gate. My foot hit it and it clinked."

She held out to the manager a large key, almost three inches long.

"The key to the gate!" the manager exclaimed. "But at night it's always kept behind the desk." He ran a hand through his hair. "But of course," he continued quickly, "anyone could obtain it. Not just a guest."

"We've got to call the police!" a short, plump man in a maroon robe said loudly. It was the guest who had led the pack to the garden.

"I don't see what that would accomplish," Miss Mitchell interrupted. "The man's gone and nothing's been taken. After all, what is Nice without a cat burglar?" And she smiled charmingly at the men.

The manager's face relaxed a little and he looked hopefully at the guests who had straggled into the garden to join in the excitement.

"That is true, *n'est-ce pas*? And, as mademoiselle says, there has been no harm done."

Nan's face tightened. "But the police should—"

Miss Mitchell broke in quite smoothly. "Perhaps if the manager wishes to report this matter he should do so, but I believe that most travelers would not wish to have their journeys interrupted. After all, what is there to tell the authorities?"

Nan started to speak and then she halted. What good would

it do? She looked at the manager and the people surrounding them. They wouldn't believe her. As for the French police—why should they take her word over that of Miss Mitchell's? And Dr. Yates wouldn't back her up. He'd just say it was ridiculous.

So the girl replied, "I don't suppose there is much to tell them," and she turned and walked toward the hotel. Her friends held back for a moment, then followed her.

12

THE SHAMBLING MAN RETURNS

Jack was waiting impatiently at the foot of the main staircase when the girls came down the next morning.

"I was wondering if you sleeping beauties would ever arrive," he said. "I've been here half an hour."

"It's only six a.m. right now, pal," Leslie moaned. "And that's quite early enough."

The boy shepherded them into the dining room. After ordering, he announced, "We need to have a council of war. There wasn't any chance to thrash anything out last night. Miss Mitchell didn't let us out of her sight once the group in the garden broke up."

Nan spread her hands out helplessly on the table. "We don't need a council, we need help."

"I know," the boy agreed. "And we're going to get it." He turned to the other girl. "Can you telephone your stepfather?"

Leslie frowned. "I don't think so, since they're traveling. But I can send a letter to Berlin. It should get there Monday."

"Today is Thursday," he said slowly. "Well, that's better than nothing. If we can just protect the professor for a few more days. It shouldn't be too hard." He dragged out a well-thumbed itinerary. "We leave this morning and for the next three days we'll be in the bus, driving down the Italian Riviera. We reach Naples on Saturday. I don't think we need to worry too much while we're in the small coastal towns. But in Naples and in Rome—"

"Rome," Nan repeated softly, and for a moment her eyes glowed in anticipation and then the worry line reappeared between her eyebrows. "I'll bet those Yugoslavians can get to Dr. Yates easily there."

"No, they won't," the boy disagreed. "That's what we're going to prevent. Look at it—Miss Mitchell must know when the kidnapping is planned. Why else was she lurking around last night? Now I bet she'll meet the shambling man before they try again. So if we watch her like a hawk and keep equally close tabs on Dr. Yates, we're sure to be in on the next try."

"Who watches the professor?" Leslie asked.

"I think I should stick close to Dr. Yates," Jack said, "because there might be a fight. Not that I was such a big deal last night, but next time I'll remember there aren't any rules. And since Nan's the only one who can recognize the shambling man, she should follow Miss Mitchell."

"What about me?" Leslie asked.

"You help Jack," Nan said. "The threat is to Dr. Yates, not Miss Mitchell, so the more on his trail, the better."

"Great!" the blonde girl exclaimed. "I like to be where the action is."

It was their second and final day in Naples and Nan congratulated herself on being assigned to watch Miss Mitchell. She sat in cool comfort in the hotel lobby, her feet on a rattan footstool, a novel open on her lap. Occasionally she turned a page to reinforce the illusion, but mostly she enjoyed the soothing sound of water falling from a circular fountain in the middle of the room.

She shook her head in sympathy for Jack and Leslie. It was at least ninety-five degrees outside—a baking, scorching day. But Dr. Yates, more interested in knowledge than comfort, was using the day to return to Pompeii. Nan couldn't imagine anything hotter than the dusty countryside where that long-ago city of pleasure stood. She glanced at her watch. They should be back any minute.

And then her mind turned a somersault. She stared tensely ahead, for standing at the desk, speaking softly to the clerk, was the shambling man. She couldn't mistake the hunch of his heavy shoulders or the thick reddish hair that grew low on his neck or the long, apelike arms that hung just a little too far down his torso. Turning her head stiffly, she saw Miss Mitchell was still in the writing room across the hall, her slender hand racing across a sheet of paper.

The girl swiveled to look at the man again. He was handing the hotel employee an envelope. The man nodded and turned to thrust it into a pigeonhole, then paused. Swinging around, he said, "Sir—" But the shambling man was already gone.

The clerk shrugged, started to put the message in its place, shrugged again, and walked slowly from behind the counter to the writing room. He stopped beside the guide and inquired, "Miss Mitchell, is it not? A message for you."

Nan sank back in her chair, torn between following the shambling man and watching the guide. But perhaps the note contained final instructions for the kidnapping of the professor.

A startled expression flashed over the woman's narrow face. "Thank you," she said quietly. She waited until the clerk returned to the desk before ripping open the envelope and pulling out the single sheet of paper. She read it swiftly, then jumped up, almost knocking over her chair. She stuffed the note and her unfinished letter into her purse and hurried to the main hall. Her heels clicking loudly on the tiled floor, she pushed through a curtain-covered archway and disappeared into the closed dining room.

Nan sped to the door and carefully peered through the drapes. The dining room lay shadowy and deserted, but the tables were set for dinner, their white coverings gleaming in the unlighted room. Miss Mitchell skirted around the tables, heading for the French doors that led to the terrace and the garden.

The girl looked back into the lobby, searching for someone—anyone she knew—but in the quiet of the late afternoon it was empty, the splashing water trilling to itself. Quickly, she yanked her pen from her purse, held up her book and turned to the copyright page. She scrawled, "Shambling man back. Miss Mitchell gone to meet him on terrace. Man is about 5'11", heavy, maybe 200 lbs., reddish hair low on neck, arms like gorilla." She stopped, thought desperately and added, "Brown suit American cut, ring on right hand." It wasn't much, but it was all she had time for.

She ran to the desk, tearing out the page as she went. "Please," she said urgently to the startled desk clerk, "give this note to Miss Whitaker." She folded it, wrote Leslie's name on the outside, and thrust it at the man. Then she raced to the curtained archway.

She didn't see an older woman standing in the shadows of an alcove in the writing room. The woman watched the girl, then looked at the note which the clerk was placing in a pigeon-hole. She waited patiently until the clerk furtively plucked a pack of cigarettes from his pocket and vanished through a side door. The woman crossed to the desk, took out Nan's note and scanned it. Her face stiffened, and then a small satisfied smile briefly touched her lips. She drew out a sheet of hotel notepaper, and in a good imitation of that scrawled nervous writing, wrote, "Shambling man back. Miss Mitchell gone with him. I'm following. Man six feet tall, very thin, stooped shoulders, widow's peak, thin black hair, guttural accent." The note was back in its resting place before the desk clerk returned.

When Nan reached the terrace, she was blinded for a moment by the hot light of the late afternoon sun. Light glittered off the graveled walks and the white statuary. Shading her eyes, she searched the garden. No one moved among the scarlet, pink and cream roses. A mother sat cheerfully in the broiling heat while her two children sailed cigar-boxes round and round a lily-filled pond.

"It's stuck!" the small boy wailed angrily. "Mine's stuck on that flower."

The woman laughed and began to poke at the little craft with a knobby stick.

Nan called out, "Did a woman with black hair pass through here?"

The matron nodded. "Yes, just a moment ago. She disappeared behind the cypress trees." And the woman pointed to the column of tall and stately trees that marked the boundary of the hotel grounds. "I think there's a path behind them that leads to the street."

"Thank you," the girl replied, and she raced along the pebble-covered walk to the dark column. She found the path at once. It lay in deep shadow between the trees and a high stone wall. Nan shivered. Cypress—the tree of the dead because once it's cut down it can't grow again. With slight revulsion, she moved up the footway. Far ahead, someone hurried on the noisy gravel. Abruptly, the even sound of the hurried steps stopped. Nan heard a scuffling noise, a half-smothered cry—and, after a long moment, the dull thud of solidly planted footfalls.

The girl swallowed hard and tiptoed on. As she rounded the curve, she hugged the scant shelter of the tapering trees. The path ended at a gate, now half-open. She could see the shambling man in the street, closing the rear door of some sort of old black van. With a satisfied expression on his face, he turned and began to walk heavily toward the gate.

Nan drew back, slipped between two of the trees and pressed against the foliage. The smell of cedar and the thick heat of the evening sun couldn't touch the core of icy fear deep within her as she listened to the man's approach.

Carefully, she bent down a limb, clutching the shiny, green leaves. The man strode past, a slight smile on his broad, thick-cheeked face, his arms swinging in rhythm. In one hand he held a hotel key, its bright yellow board clearly visible.

When the man was out of sight, she pushed through the trees to the path, drawn against her will to the gate and the street beyond. That room key could mean only one thing. Somehow or other, he and Miss Mitchell had done it—they'd kidnapped Dr. Yates. The professor was in that van and the man, for some reason, was on his way to the professor's room.

At the gate, the girl slowly surveyed the street. Where was Miss Mitchell? Now that she'd finished the job, had she walked away, a carefree tourist, to explore the narrow, twisting streets of Naples? The girl didn't see her. A blind beggar stood directly across the way, his head turned uncertainly in the direction of the vehicle and a puzzled look on his face. He hadn't seen anything, Nan knew, but he'd heard something.

She looked at what she'd thought was a van and involuntarily backed away. It was an old black hearse with humpy fenders and high roof. Curtains masked the long side windows.

In there, she thought, in there.

The handle of the door felt dirty and sticky in her hand. She pulled it down and the door swung out. A sweet, sickish smell almost made her gag. In the dark interior of the cavernous hearse, she could dimly see a covered form stretched out on the ramp where . . . her mind refused to say it. But why was he so still, so inert? As she grappled with a new fear, she heard the distant scuff of someone moving on the graveled path.

Her instinct was to escape—to run down the street. No, walk, her terrified mind told her. The shambling man didn't know her. She'd just be an American girl strolling on a picturesque lane. She could run as soon as the hearse was out of sight. Hurry to the hotel and get help.

But it would be too late then. Dr. Yates would be gone.

The girl clung tightly to the handle. The footsteps were nearer. In only a moment the big man would be at the center of the curving trees and he'd see her. Feverishly she began to push the rear door shut—and again she saw that still body.

He wasn't her responsibility! No, but that summer evening in Montmartre she had chosen to follow the guide—and this was where the trail ended.

So many times, when she hadn't wanted to face the ultimate end of a course she'd set, her mother had said lightly but firmly, "In for a penny, in for a pound, Nan."

In for a penny, in for a pound.

She pulled the door wide again and climbed unsteadily into the hearse. With fumbling hands, she drew the panel shut behind her. Dropping to the floor and suppressing a shudder, she squeezed into the only hiding place—the space between the coffin ramp and the floor.

In the absolute darkness of the curtained interior, she lay stiffly, almost sick from the stuffy, fetid air and the fear that swirled through her. When the door swung open, she curled herself more tightly. Would some scrap of color from her dress betray her?

The van floor rocked as the man slung two suitcases inside, then slammed the door. In a moment she heard him climb into the front seat. The motor roared. The hearse began to move.

13

A COMPLETE SURPRISE

Rattling noisily, the vehicle hurtled along, its chassis swaying as the wheels bumped and thumped over rough streets and careened around sharp corners. The sweet sickening smell, which struck her when she'd first opened the rear door, grew stronger and more overpowering in the narrow space. There was so little air, so little air, she thought dizzily. And then she struggled with a new terror—she couldn't breathe. Weakly, Nan forced herself to roll from beneath the mounted slab.

Pulling herself up to her knees, she rested against the hot metal side of the hearse. The driver yanked sharply and picked up speed, throwing her off-balance. She fell on her side and desperately began to scrabble up again. The odor was getting worse. It couldn't be carbon monoxide, she thought. That deadly gas has no odor.

She seemed to be moving in slow motion. When her hand brushed against the damp rag, she thrust it away. But maybe it would help. Something wet. Searching the floor, she found the cloth, raised it to her face, then quickly flung it down. That damp rag was saturated with chloroform. Dimly, she remembered the day in general science when the teacher had used just a drop to anesthetize a white rat—too much chloroform was deadly. How much had been used to slow the breathing of the still form beside her? She had to get rid of the rag and let in some fresh air.

Nan pulled upright and fumbled with the curtain masking the window. It was sewn tightly to thin bars above and below and couldn't be moved. She managed to push her hand up between the lower bar and the frame. Pawing up and down, she realized with despair that the glass sat solidly in its frame. She stumbled toward the rear door, lost her footing and crashed down on all fours.

A thin stream of fresh air struck her face. Free of chloroform, it was as exhilarating as the first chill of autumn. Flattening against the floor, she stuck her nose up against the small crack, where the door didn't fit in its frame securely, and breathed deeply. As her head cleared, she faced what she had to do—get the rag and throw it out. But the hearse was racing along a winding road. If her exhausted arms didn't hold tightly enough, the thrust of the wind would rip the handle from her fingers—and probably send her flying onto the road.

There had to be a way. She turned back into the interior of the swaying vehicle and reached out. Something was holding the prisoner on that platform! She slid her hand along the side of the slab and her fingers touched the grainy roughness of rope. If there was just an extra length. Dropping to the floor, she felt around with her hands. The coil lay in the right front corner. Grabbing it, she crawled back to the door and knotted one end around its handle and the other around the nearest metal upright supporting the coffin rest.

She braced one hand against the roof and twisted the handle with the other. The door ripped away from its frame, but stopped with a sharp jerk when the rope played out. Air swept inside. Nan watched tensely as the cord tightened and strained, but it held. Clutching the curtain rod of the side window, she looked out.

The sun hung low in the west, a fiery golden orange, changing the vivid blue of the ocean to jade green. Instinctively, her grasp tightened as the hearse careened around a hairpin curve. Just past the screeching whine of the tires, the roadside fell away in a sheer drop. Over the rattle of the fenders and the wheeze of the motor, she could hear breakers crashing to shore. Well, at least now she knew roughly where they were—on a coastal road, traveling south of Naples. Not that the knowledge was exactly helpful.

Abruptly, the hearse slowed and its horn sounded angrily. The sudden decrease in speed sent the back door spinning toward its frame. Nan lunged forward and caught it just in time. If it had crashed shut, even the rattling progress of the vehicle wouldn't have masked the noise. She didn't dare to leave it open and unattended while she searched for the chloroform-doused cloth. She closed the door and stood once again in absolute darkness. On her hands and knees, she blindly searched for the rag. She found it—moist and sticky and completely repugnant. Holding her breath, she hurried back to the door, opened it and flung the cloth out.

Now that the dangerous source of the fumes was removed, she had to help the professor. She shut the door again and moved carefully on the swaying floor to the slab and gently reached out her hand.

A sudden deluge of ice water couldn't have shocked her more. Her fingers tingled in disbelief as they brushed fine, silky hair. Lightly, she touched a petal-soft cheek.

It wasn't the professor after all, she realized quickly. Lying there unconscious was Miss Mitchell! Nan bent nervously to the immobile face. She sighed in relief as she saw that Miss Mitchell was still breathing faintly.

Nan stood up, uncertain and frightened, oblivious to the swaying movement of the hearse. What had happened? She tried desperately to think. Her mind held on to one solid fact. The shambling man was the enemy. This she knew without doubt. He'd been the one who'd landed so quietly and purposefully on Dr. Yates' balcony in Nice. So if the shambling man kidnapped Miss Mitchell, that meant that the girl and the guide were on the same side.

Her fingers hesitated for a moment above the ropes binding Miss Mitchell. Then she shrugged and began to tug on a stiff knot. She couldn't leave Miss Mitchell in the hands of that man.

No matter how hard she pulled, the knot wouldn't slip. Finally she stopped, her fingers rubbed sore by the abrasive rope. Somewhere in the inky darkness there should be a tool she could use to cut the rope. She knelt, began to pat the floor, and found a metal box almost immediately. She gingerly began to poke within. One by one she traced the outline of a screwdriver, hammer, wrench . . . and a file. It was almost a foot long. Its ridged sides should make short work of the rope,

The hearse slowed its furious pace.

Nan had been so involved in looking for something to cut the rope with that she hadn't noticed the deceleration for a moment. And then she stiffened. The van braked almost to a stop, then swung sharply right. It shuddered and shook as the driver cautiously guided it down a steep and twisting incline. Nan scrambled for the door, still clutching the file. She had to remove that cord from the door handle before the vehicle stopped. Curling her left hand around the curtain rod and bracing her body with her feet, she nudged the point of the tool into the knot around the handle and pried. It gave a little. She gritted her teeth and rasped the file back and forth. The knot loosened and the rope fell free.

Nan held onto the cord and pulled her way back to the coffin rest where the other end of the rope was tied. The hearse jolted to a stop. The driver's door opened—then slammed.

Carefully, slowly, she raised the file again. Her throat ached with fear, but her hands were steady. She edged the tip of the tool between the strands and wrenched it back and forth. The rope gave. Ripping it away from the support, she flung herself beneath the coffin rest as the rear door of the van began to open.

The floor rocked as the heavy man climbed into the hearse. He switched on a flashlight, beaming it down on his unconscious prisoner. Nan lay rigid, staring at his shoes. The highly polished leather gleamed in the light. He stood there for a moment, then abruptly turned, climbed out of the van, slammed the door—and locked it.

Nan slumped. Until that final chilling click, she had held onto hope—a rather worn hope, maybe, but it had helped to carry her forward. She lay on the dirty floor, one hand holding the file, and rubbing her eyes with the other.

In the utter quiet following the rattling ride, she heard the guide's light, wispy breathing. Nan's hand tightened on the tool. With great effort she rolled out of her hiding place, stood up and began to work on Miss Mitchell's bonds. The young woman stirred as Nan reached the third knot. Moaning softly, the prisoner rolled her head from side to side.

"Sick," she mumbled. "So sick."

Nan stopped and leaned close to the slab. "Miss Mitchell, Miss Mitchell." She waited. The woman was breathing more deeply. Suddenly her hand moved and clutched Nan's arm. Nan whispered, "Please, please don't cry out. Please."

She felt the woman's fear subside. The intensity of her plea had registered in Miss Mitchell's half-conscious mind.

Nan bent closer still and repeated, "Don't be frightened. It's Nan. Lie still while I finish untying you. Keep on breathing deeply."

Quickly, Nan sliced through the last knot and pulled the ropes away.

"Miss Mitchell, do you think you can sit up?"

"I'll try," Miss Mitchell answered weakly.

Nan caught her around the shoulders and gently helped her up.

"My head hurts," the guide moaned. "And I'm—oh—"

She swung her head away from the girl, leaned over the edge of the table, and began to be sick. Nan swallowed hard. She mustn't be sick too, she mustn't. Breathing in gasps, the guide finally straightened up.

"Sorry," she murmured. "Everything went alleyoop."

"It's the chloroform," the girl said.

The woman shook her head slowly. "What happened?"

"The shambling man kidnapped you," Nan replied.

"Who?" the woman asked.

"A big, awkward man. He followed you that night in Montmartre when you met the fellow wearing the railroad cap." She felt Miss Mitchell grow tense beside her.

"He followed me—" the guide repeated blankly. "But how did you know that?"

"I was trailing you, too," Nan continued uneasily. "I was the one on the fire escape that the woman was screaming about."

"And why were you spying on me?" Miss Mitchell inquired in a level tone.

Nan paused and her old hostility came back. “Because you’re in on a plot to kidnap Dr. Yates.” Miss Mitchell started to interrupt, but Nan rushed on. “No, I know all about it. I overheard you talking to Dr. Yates on the ship and then my roommate and I got a letter from her stepfather, a newspaperman, telling us that he’d heard a rumor Yugoslavian agents were going to kidnap Dr. Yates.

“And I thought you were working with the shambling man, because he was the one who tried to get the professor that night in Nice. So today when he left the note for you at the hotel, I followed you. When I saw the hearse, I was sure you’d finally managed to kidnap Dr. Yates.”

For a moment Miss Mitchell said absolutely nothing and then she asked incredulously, “You thought that I and this—shambling man were working together to kidnap Dr. Yates?”

“You’re some sort of Yugoslavian agent, aren’t you?” Nan demanded. “I don’t understand why the shambling man took you, but please, I’ve helped you now. You can’t harm the professor.”

Miss Mitchell began to laugh weakly.

“I don’t see what’s so funny,” Nan said.

Miss Mitchell stopped laughing abruptly. “I’m sorry,” she said. “You’re quite right to be angry. There’s nothing funny about it. And when I think of the time we’ve both wasted—” She broke off, her voice discouraged. Then with sudden resolution she began to speak in her usual tone. “Enough of this. Let me assure you that we’re on the same side. When we have a moment, I’ll explain it all. But right now we’re wasting time. We’ve got to find some way out of this mess. First, do you have any idea where we are?”

“On a beach somewhere south of Naples,” Nan answered quickly.

"A beach," Miss Mitchell said. "Well, we aren't here to play in the sun. It sounds like a boat trip."

"We couldn't go all the way to Yugoslavia from here, could we?"

"I don't have any idea. I don't even know why we're here, so I can't guess where we're going. The point is not to go." Miss Mitchell stood up, grabbing the girl for support,

"We'd better check the windows of this thing and see if we can open them."

"I've already done that," Nan replied.

"Hmm. And the door's locked."

"Yes."

"Then we'll have to break a window."

"The tool chest!" Nan pulled out a hammer and a hefty wrench. "These should do," she said, and she turned toward the window, ready to break it.

"Wait!" Miss Mitchell warned. "Where did you put that file?"

Nan stooped by the slab and found it.

Miss Mitchell took the file and quickly slit an opening in the curtains. Pulling back a loose flap of material, she peered into the night. After the total darkness of the van, the moonlit beach was easily visible. A headland thrust its way into the sea about twenty yards to their right. The narrow beach, strewn with large boulders, hugged the base of the rugged incline which the hearse had driven down. Nothing moved but the foaming surf. She kept her hand lightly on Nan's arm as she carefully surveyed the scene again. Finally she sighed and shook her head.

"There he is," she said.

Nan followed Miss Mitchell's finger, but she saw nothing. "Watch," Miss Mitchell insisted. Nan stared at a huge black boulder which jutted up from the beach, dwarfing the slender thread of sand. And then she saw the tiny red flame. It was the glowing tip of a cigarette. It meant defeat.

Slowly Nan lowered her arm. “So the window idea is out,” she said.

Miss Mitchell didn’t answer for a moment. In the dim moonlight, Nan could see her intent frown. “We’ve got one chance,” said Miss Mitchell finally. “It isn’t much, but it’s better than nothing. When he comes back, we’ll be waiting on either side of the door. There’s no reason he shouldn’t swing it wide open. When he does, we’ll throw the wrench and hammer at him and then scramble out of here as fast as we can. Okay? And then run like fury up that road and try to find cover.”

“We can try it,” Nan replied. She paused. “But how can you run? You’re still pretty wobbly.”

“Wobbly or not, there’s a lot at stake. And it’s marvelous what adrenaline can do.”

They stood at either side of the door, Nan clutching her hammer in a moist palm, Miss Mitchell holding the wrench.

“And now,” Miss Mitchell said, “we wait.”

14

FAREWELL TO ITALY

"How long do you think it'll be?" Nan asked.

Her companion shrugged, then leaned over to pat the girl on the arm. "There's no way to know, so try and relax."

"Miss Mitchell," Nan began tentatively a little later. "You said we were on the same side and you'd explain."

Miss Mitchell sat quietly for a moment. Finally she spoke. "All right. Of course part of this I'm not supposed to disclose, but you know so much already and you're in a tight spot because of me, so here goes. I laughed a while ago because it's so ironic that you thought I was in on Dr. Yates' kidnapping. You see, I was supposed to be protecting him."

"Then you're an American agent!" Nan exclaimed.

"Not an accredited one," the guide said. "I was keeping an eye on him unofficially. I'm an executive secretary at the CIA. The rumor that Yugoslavian agents were planning to kidnap Dr. Yates came to my boss. He thought it was so unlikely that Yugoslavia would plot to steal an American that he didn't feel he could spare an agent to keep an eye on things. But it was time for my vacation anyway and he asked if I'd go along on the tour and watch for anything peculiar." She laughed. "I left for New York soon after we received the tip."

"Oh," Nan breathed slowly. "Then it was arranged that you take Mrs. Stimson's place. And at the museum—"

"I was picking up some last-minute instructions on how to contact a CIA man in Paris."

"But why did you go through my bags on the ship?" Nan asked.

"I was a little suspicious of the way you kept popping up," she replied. "But how did you know I searched your luggage?"

"One of my cabinmates saw you leaving our quarters. Everything that happened made me more convinced that you were a Yugoslavian agent. I was sure you and the shambling man were working together when you stopped the hotel manager in Nice from calling the police."

"I was just afraid that the Yugoslavians would find out the CIA knew about the plot," Miss Mitchell explained. "But I reported it later to the French Secret Service so they could conduct a quiet investigation. You see, that incident in Nice really surprised me. All our information had indicated the kidnapping would take place in Trieste."

"I guess I could never make a living as a spy," the guide continued. "I suppose Dr. Yates had a point. He kept insisting he could take care of himself. It hurt his manhood that a woman was supposed to be protecting him." She paused and added, "And he's such a nice guy. We would have liked each other." She became brisk again. "Anyway, he was right. I fell completely for the phony note the shambling man left, saying the professor was in trouble and I should hurry up the cypress path to the street. In fact, I've got to admit that I'm just not cut out for this sort of thing. The most ridiculous part is that I'm the one they kidnapped—and I don't have any idea why."

"Maybe they found out you were a CIA agent and decided to kidnap you."

"But why? Because they don't like CIA agents?" the woman suggested wryly. "I'm sure they don't, but kidnapping doesn't help that. My boss never did think it made sense that they'd want to kidnap Dr. Yates, but he did concede there could be some strange reason. But I'm not Dr. Yates. I couldn't possibly know whatever it is he's supposed to know. Sometimes I agree with Neal—I mean Dr. Yates—that the whole thing's a fantasy."

Nan balanced the hammer in her hand. "But it's real. The shambling man is real. We're prisoners in a hearse on a little beach. It has to mean something!"

"Yes," Miss Mitchell replied with the first sign of fear Nan had heard in her voice. "It does have to mean something. I only wish—"

She fell silent as a harsh clattering warned that another vehicle was coming down the steep incline to the beach. The machine rattled to a stop nearby, and a door slammed.

"Steven!" a man called loudly.

"Shut your mouth!" a voice in an American accent snapped. So the shambling man was an American, after all.

"Do you want the world to hear?" he demanded.

Nan and Miss Mitchell pressed close to the small gap in the curtain.

Their captor stood beside a black Peugot, looming over a smaller man. After their first loud exchange, they spoke too softly for the prisoners to hear. But it was clear that the newcomer's message wasn't welcome. Their captor, Steven, the shambling man, shook his head angrily, then shrugged his shoulders and pointed up toward the highway.

The other man shrugged, too, then climbed into the car. As it strained up the incline, Steven moved past the boulders and stared out to sea.

"What do you suppose that was all about?" Miss Mitchell mused.

"Maybe they're looking for us already," Nan suggested.

"I don't think so," her companion replied, and she let the flap of curtain fall back into place.

The prisoners sat down again on the flooring and began to wait in silence. Nan slumped against the metal siding.

How long they waited she didn't know. Fifteen minutes . . . twenty . . . or perhaps only five. Time moved so slowly in that small black space.

Miss Mitchell touched her hand to warn her, but she heard it, too. The soft shushing sound of someone approaching over sand.

"He's coming," Miss Mitchell whispered. "Get ready!"

They stood and pressed against the sides of the van. Nan wished the empty feeling in her chest would go away. When the key twisted in the lock, she took a deep breath, tensed her knees, and drew back her lifted arm.

Steven swung the door fully open and had just begun to move forward when the prisoners threw their weapons and lunged. Nan heard him grunt in surprise and pain as her hammer smashed into his shoulder. He reeled back and lost his footing. Jumping onto the sand, Nan ran past the hearse as if a band of devils were nipping at her footsteps.

"What the—" Steven cried. And then there was a thrashing noise and a thud. Nan skidded to a stop. Miss Mitchell hadn't been fast enough. She heard Miss Mitchell cry, "Run! Run! Get—" The shout was abruptly muffled.

Nan drew a breath and began to scramble up the side of the

hill, brambles clutching at her legs, rocks and stones sliding beneath her feet. No one pursued her, but what was happening on that isolated beach? She stumbled among low oak branches. This was impossible. She had to find her way to the twisting road that led down to the beach. She halted and took a precious moment to look desperately around. Through the scrubby, twisted trees, she saw a swath of moonlight. Altering her course, she ran toward the light and reached the road. She half-ran, half-fell up the narrow lane, but she began to feel a spark of hope. No one was after her and she could hear the sound of cars whizzing past. The highway was so near and no one was—

The brawny arm encircled her neck like a vise and jerked her backward off her feet. For a terrified moment she fought and struggled. Then she realized it was useless. Panting and off-balance, she stood still.

No wonder Steven hadn't chased her. He knew his friend would be up the hill. She and Miss Mitchell had been trapped at every turn, the girl thought bitterly. She gave no resistance when Steven's friend turned her roughly around and herded her down the uneven rocky lane.

"Well, Steven, you won't be delayed after all," the man said.

Nan frowned as he spoke, but she couldn't place his accent. English was certainly not his native tongue, but he didn't speak it as an Italian or Frenchman would.

Her thoughts broke off when Steven flashed a torch directly in her eyes, then snapped it off.

"How did you know about me?" he demanded.

She was filled with fear when she heard the cold anger in his voice. She flinched as he moved closer. "Why did you leave a note describing me at the hotel?"

Nan stood there dumbly. How did he know about the note? How could he know?

"Answer me!" The big man grabbed her wrist.

"I thought you were a friend of Miss Mitchell's," she gasped. "I saw you follow her in Paris."

His grip didn't slacken. "And who did you think I was?" he asked.

"A Yugoslavian agent." Her arm was laced with pain.

He released her abruptly, and she thought he smiled slightly. Then his face hardened again. "You shouldn't have pried. You know too much now."

The other man broke into a torrent of words in a language Nan had never heard before. It wasn't French or Italian or Spanish or German. Out of the corner of her eye, she saw Miss Mitchell stiffen. Then the woman's face grew blank and she relaxed a little.

Steven listened impatiently. Finally he interrupted. "I don't care what she said. What use will they have for the girl over there?"

The big man turned and looked coldly at Nan. The silence grew until it was a heavy, leaden thing. The tension didn't lessen when Steven asked the other man a short question in the strange language and gestured toward the ocean.

Frightened and bewildered, Nan turned toward Miss Mitchell and saw horror in her eyes.

The other man shook his head violently.

Steven shrugged his shoulders. "All right, I'll take her along and let him decide."

Nan closed her eyes and felt relief washing over her, leaving her limp. She didn't know what Steven had suggested, and she didn't want to know. Instinctively, she moved closer to Miss Mitchell. She gave a small gasp when she saw that the guide was supporting her left arm with her right hand.

"What's wrong?" she asked softly. "Did he hurt you?"

"A little," the young woman replied, "when he grabbed me. But don't worry, it's not broken." She lapsed into silence again.

Steven briefly flicked on the flashlight to check his watch. He turned to his confederate. "Bring some rope from the hearse," he ordered, "and don't forget the suitcases."

When the other man returned, Steven said, "Tie the girl's hands. I'll take care of Miss Mitchell."

Nan didn't struggle when the man twisted the rope around her wrists. The hemp scratched her skin. She saw Miss Mitchell wince when Steven grabbed her arms.

"Don't!" Nan called out. "Her arm's hurt. Don't tie her up."

"That's Miss Mitchell's problem," Steven replied indifferently.

Nan started to protest, but gave up when Miss Mitchell shook her head.

And then came the sound she had half-consciously awaited, the purring roar of a motorboat.

Steven whirled toward the water, flashed his light twice briefly and motioned to the prisoners. "This way," he ordered, as matter-of-fact as an elevator operator.

They trudged through the soft sand with the other man bringing up the rear. Crossing the beach, the men and their prisoners edged along a narrow path at the base of the headland. Nan tried to keep her balance on the slippery, wet rocks. Waves crashed into the cliff beneath them, throwing up a fine spray. If she fell, with her hands tied in front of her. . . .

She didn't look up until the others had stopped. Steven led Miss Mitchell out onto a small, narrow pier whose dark and weathered pilings would be almost invisible from the beach in daylight.

Its motor chugging softly, the boat nosed alongside the pier and held steady. Steven swung Miss Mitchell over the side. The man at the wheel caught her by the elbow, then shoved her into a back seat. Then Steven pulled Nan forward, lifted her roughly, and dropped her next to Miss Mitchell.

Stepping back to the center of the small pier, he turned to his friend. "Take the hearse back," he ordered, reaching into his pocket for the keys. "And make a report about our extra passenger."

The man took the keys, then said sharply, "The passport! You've forgotten the passport."

Steven whirled about. "Miss Mitchell, your purse," he demanded.

"Certainly," she replied. She picked it up awkwardly with her bound hands, and then quickly hurled it as far as she could. For an instant no one moved. A sharp plop sounded as the purse hit the water. Nan bent and grabbed her own pocketbook, but Steven was too quick for her. Pinning her arm to the back of his seat, he wrenched the bag from her hand and tossed it onto the pier.

The big man slowly stooped and picked up the purse. He drew out her blue passport and tossed the bag at her feet.

He spoke angrily. "That was a stupid thing to do, Miss Mitchell. It's very dangerous to disobey us."

He angrily thrust Nan's passport into his pocket, and picked up Miss Mitchell's suitcases.

"I don't believe our chief'll be pleased at what's happened tonight," the other man said, enjoying his superior's uneasiness.

"Get going," Steven ordered. He turned away from the other and stepped into the boat. "Let's get out of here," he commanded.

The engine throbbed and the boat swung out into the cove, heading for open sea. The sleek hull lifted high out of the water as the craft roared ahead, faster and faster. Pushed deep into her seat by the whipping air, Nan twisted to look over her shoulder at the coastline of Italy. She watched until the last twinkling light disappeared.

15

DUE EAST

The boat skimmed through the water, traveling so fast it was hard to breathe. The spray cut by the speeding vessel covered them with a fine mist. Damp and miserable, Nan huddled down in her seat, seeking any scrap of warmth. The night air off the ocean held no hint of the steaming heat which had enveloped Naples that day.

"We're going awfully fast, aren't we?" Nan asked.

"Yes," Miss Mitchell replied calmly. "About forty miles an hour, maybe even faster. When they call this a speedboat, they mean it."

"If we crash or something . . ." and Nan's voice trailed off as she gazed out over the dark, empty sea.

"Relax," Miss Mitchell said quietly. "This fellow knows how to handle her."

Nan stared at Miss Mitchell. Propped against the side of the boat, the tour guide looked as comfortable as if she were on a pleasure outing.

"How can you be so—so casual?" Nan asked.

"There's no point in sitting here worrying all the way to nowhere. We can't do anything until we know what's going on, so we might as well enjoy what we can. After all, what happens next may not be—" She broke off, then continued quickly, "I love boats. My family used to spend a part of every summer in Minnesota and we had one very much like this. A nineteen-footer that could ride the wind." She lapsed into silence.

"I see," Nan replied slowly and then tried to relax in her seat. Closing her eyes, she listened to the *whoosh* of the boat sliding smoothly through the water. By degrees, calm flowed through her, bolstering her self-confidence. They weren't beaten yet.

She opened her eyes and stared up at the stars. She wondered what Jack and Leslie were doing now. Had they already sounded an alarm or would they be nervously waiting for her to return to the hotel? By midnight at the latest, she was sure they'd call for help. But what good would it do? The matron in the hotel garden had seen her pass by, but only a blind beggar had stood in the narrow little street where the hearse waited. By morning the search would be on for her and Miss Mitchell, but it wouldn't do any good to hunt for them in Italy. As the boat continued to slice through the sea, her optimism dwindled.

When the craft finally slowed to a stop, Nan looked in every direction. The moonlight shone on an empty world of moving water.

The shambling man leaned over the windshield, lifted up a steel anchor and slowly let it down into the water.

"At least," Nan said softly to Miss Mitchell, "we aren't going all the way across the Mediterranean in this. I'd be frozen by then." She tried to make it a joke, but she was aching with cold.

"It looks as though we're going to meet someone here," Miss Mitchell answered.

"Soon, I hope," Nan said, bunching her knees up to her chest to get a little more warmth. "Anything's better than this."

The boat seemed to rock interminably in the swells. The big man turned on his flashlight several times to peer at his watch.

At first the soft hum didn't mean anything to Nan but when it turned into a throb she sat up sharply and scanned the night sky. An airplane!

The shambling man opened a compartment and drew out a box about eight inches high and five inches wide. He balanced it in his lap, and she heard shutters click rapidly. Light flashed spasmodically from the little machine. He was signaling the airplane!

The safety lights of the plane shone like brightly colored stars. The sound of the engine filled the night. Briefly a light flashed twice high above them.

"Here it comes," the driver said with relief.

"Late," the American answered. "I was beginning to worry." As he spoke, he turned the light of his signal straight up into the sky to guide the plane.

Nan watched, puzzled. What was the craft going to do? The roar of the engine was almost on top of them. The plane glided closer and closer to the waves. When it landed, water foamed and it skimmed along the top of the sea. The aquaplane came to rest, rolling in the swells, about thirty yards from them.

"Let's go," the shambling man ordered, switching off the lamp and pulling up the anchor.

When the boat drew alongside the aircraft, he threw a rope to the pilot, who was leaning out of the open cockpit door. He slipped the cord around a strut of the pontoon.

"Miss Mitchell first," the big man directed. "Step carefully." He helped her onto the pontoon and the pilot guided her up two steps into the cockpit.

Nan's legs felt rubbery and weak when she stood. The boat surged up and down and she could hear the water sucking and hissing. She hated the strong grasp of her captor when he lifted and swung her onto the pontoon. Her feet slipped on its wet slick surface, but the pilot caught her by the shoulder and pulled her up. Then he carried the suitcases on board. Nan sat in a rear seat next to Miss Mitchell. Their kidnapper swung aboard and strapped the seat belts. As the safety harness jerked tight, she heard the motorboat roar away—their last link with Italy.

The engine of the plane revved up and the craft pulled across the water, straining to lift into the sky. Too soon, the ocean was below them. The aquaplane banked, turned and settled on a steady course.

In the unpressurized plane, the deafening noise of the engine deadened her mind. She leaned back and didn't try to think or plan. And she tried very hard not to feel. She attempted to shut away the thought of her mother and father. She wondered if even now in Ethiopia some American official was calling to say, "Awfully sorry, sir. I'm afraid we have some bad news. . . ."

Her mother—she half-smiled as she pressed her cheek against the cold, grainy upholstery of the seat. Her dear, sweet mother, who believed implicitly in good and in reason. All through the years, when Nan had any sort of problem she'd gone to her. In a gentle, even voice, she'd always insisted, "There's *some* sort of solution to every problem. Think, Nan."

But not this time, Mother, the girl said softly to herself. "Not this time," she repeated aloud.

Miss Mitchell leaned closer, saying, "Louder. I can't hear you over the roar."

"I—" Nan hesitated. "I wonder where we are going?" she asked finally.

"East," Miss Mitchell replied. "Due east."

East, Nan thought. Eastward lay the peninsula of Italy, the Adriatic Sea—and Yugoslavia. Millions of stars, the ones never seen in a city, glittered in the sky, as beautiful and distant as any hope of safety.

Not this time, she said to herself again, slumping in her seat. But at least the cabin was warm and dry and she was so very tired. She drifted off into an uneasy sleep, her head cramped against the cushion, her bunched hands cramped in front of her. She slept fitfully, but always when she awakened for a moment, she could hear the pounding din of the motor.

Nan rocked her head to and fro. She didn't want to wake up. "Leave me alone," she muttered. "Leave me alone." But the regular punching on her shoulder didn't stop. Opening her eyes, she looked around in a daze. That awful noise, she thought, what is it? She tried to move and something held her. First she felt sudden terror. Then she remembered.

Groggily, she realized that Miss Mitchell was bumping her shoulder. Miss Mitchell leaned close and said. "Wake up. We're landing."

Nan jerked around to peer out the window. It was still dark but she knew the guide was right, for the plane was steadily losing altitude.

"Have I been asleep long?" she asked.

Miss Mitchell shook her head. "About two hours."

"Are we in Yugoslavia already?" Nan inquired.

Miss Mitchell slowly shook her head. "No. At least not yet."

She broke off as the aquaplane struck the water, jolting them back into their seats. Gradually the craft lost speed and maneuvered next to a dock.

In the sudden silence after the pilot turned off the ignition, Nan said, "At least there won't be any more boat rides."

Steven looked back at her. "No, this is the end of the line—for now."

When he unstrapped her seat belt, her fatigue gave her courage to ask coolly, "Don't you suppose you could cut off the ropes? We can't very well escape."

He laughed. "No, I guess you can't. All right." He pulled a penknife from his pocket and sliced through the hemp.

"Thank you," she said. She was grateful. He could have refused. Her wrists were rubbed raw from the prickly bonds, but it was wonderful to move her stiff, cramped arms.

And it was a relief to be out of the plane, standing on the pier. Steven walked between them to the end of the dock where a path curved up a fir-covered hill. A soft breeze was filled with the mingled scent of wild mint and jasmine. The path wound through a grove of tall, straight pines and then angled sharply into a carefully cultivated rose garden. The sweet smell of the roses contrasted oddly with the crunch of gravel in the stillness of early morning.

A square two-story villa, similar in style to those which dotted the hills of the Italian and French Rivieras, loomed at the end of the garden. A light shone from a ground floor window.

Steven guided them to a huge rear door. Twice he sounded a massive iron knocker shaped like a ram's head. In a moment the door swung inward. An old woman in a white yoked blouse and a long, dark-red skirt almost touching the floor stood back to let them enter. She motioned down a deep hall and spoke to Steven in the same guttural language Nan had first heard on the beach. A Yugoslavian dialect?

As the man shepherded them down the wide corridor, Nan looked about her curiously. The passageway was lit by sconces set in the wall every few feet, which threw into bright relief the pale rose of the stuccoed walls. The highly waxed wood floors were handpegged. Bright flashes of dark blues and rich reds intermingled in an occasional oriental throw-rug.

While their captor knocked on the door at the end of the hall, Nan looked at an intricately carved oaken stairway that curved out of sight to her right. To the left, another wide hall led toward the front of the villa.

"Come in." An urbane voice called from inside. An English accent, yet tinged by foreign intonation.

Opening the door, their captor stood aside for the prisoners to enter. The long, wide room exuded color. A brilliant red rug covered the floor. Bookshelves lined one wall. Dim tapestries of soft purple hung from another. Oyster-gray drapes swathed the French windows opposite the hall door. In the precise center of the room, sat an immense rosewood desk. Behind it, dwarfed a little by the splendor, sat a middle-aged man with thinning black hair. The features in his face seemed etched in stone.

The shambling man closed the big wooden door. Their host stared silently at them for a moment, then said, "I wasn't expecting *two* guests, Steven."

The words were mild, but Nan could see sweat glistening on Steven's broad, ruddy forehead.

"It's not my fault," he replied defensively. But as he attempted to explain, he stumbled over his words. His voice trailed off as the other man made no response.

Their host eased back in his chair and placed his fingertips together. His hands were long, slender and graceful. But altogether distasteful, Nan thought.

"Not your fault?" the man repeated. "You should not have been observed in Paris." He leaned forward. "But there'll be time to discuss that later. Give me their passports." He stretched out one of his delicate hands. Nan felt almost sorry for Steven. His face tightened and he swallowed.

"The girl's," he muttered, thrusting the thin blue document forward. "The other one threw hers in the ocean."

The air in the room seemed to congeal as anger flushed the leader's thin ridged face. He began to speak icily in the language which the small man on the beach had used. Nan glanced at Miss Mitchell, and again she saw a startled look, quickly suppressed. The woman's face was blank, but her eyes were bright and watchful.

Steven kept shaking his head as his superior addressed him. At last the man fell silent. He looked at the two prisoners and then shrugged. "It'll mean a delay. But I think our Miss Jones"—he glanced slyly at the captives "—was correct in sending the girl, too. She may be quite useful." He laughed and it was rather like a horse whinnying. Nan didn't see the humor, and she liked him even less than she'd first thought.

The expression of sly humor slipped from his face, and he waved his hands as if he were shooing pigeons away. "Show our guests to their room, Steven. We've got work to do."

The shambling American gestured for them to come, but when they rose, Miss Mitchell walked to the desk instead. The man looked up irritably.

"Am I to understand," she asked evenly, "that we're prisoners of Yugoslavia?"

Again the high whinny came from his pale thin lips. "Ah yes, of course, Miss Mitchell. That's precisely what you're to understand." He laughed again.

She studied him for a moment, started to speak and then changed her mind.

"Good evening," she said quietly. Turning toward the door, she added, "Come, Nan. It's been a long day."

16

FRIGHTFULLY CLEVER

Nan stirred drowsily. She tried to slip back into sleep, but the hoarse squawk of seagulls shredded the morning. The constant dull boom of the surf crashing to shore helped to waken her. Opening her eyes, she looked around. Sunshine streamed through the open windows. A warm summer breeze ruffled the lacy white curtains. In the bright morning light, the waxed wooden floors gleamed. Even the heavy dark furniture with its ornate moldings reflected a polished patina.

Her glance swung slowly back to the windows. They framed a brilliantly blue sky. Suddenly she was wide awake. No bars blocked her view. She lay quite still. Was there a guard outside?

Not really daring to hope, Nan pushed back a light quilt, slipped out of bed and padded across the room, the floor cool under her feet. She stopped short at the window, her hand tightly clutching the sill. The little spark of hope withered and died. She gazed down the sheer drop at a long wave sparkling in the sun.

It surged against jagged black rocks to foam and splinter into a million iridescent drops.

No wonder the windows weren't barred. This portion of the villa perched at the very edge of a stark cliff. The narrow ribbon of beach was a long, long way down. To her right, she could see part of the rose garden through which they'd walked the night before. Beyond the flowers, dark-green fir trees mantled the ground as it sloped toward the sea. A solid pier jutted into the water. Nearby, a motorboat bobbed in the water. The aquaplane was gone. She scanned the sea. All the way to the horizon, it was empty.

Nan sighed and turned back to survey the room. Miss Mitchell was still asleep in the old four-poster they'd shared, her black hair ruffled on the pillow, her face serene. Nan wished she'd wake up. She had a million questions.

The night before, Steven had guided them up the stairs to this corner room, unlocking it with a key hanging on a hook next to the door. Once the lock clicked shut and the man's footsteps retreated down the hall, Nan had rushed into speech, but the woman had cut her off with a weary shake of her head.

"Let it lie until morning," Miss Mitchell interrupted. "We're dead on our feet and we won't accomplish anything by hashing it around and staying up for another hour."

The young woman drew out two nightgowns from her luggage. She handed one to Nan. Stumbling with fatigue, the girl shed her crumpled clothes, put on the gown and climbed gratefully into bed, aware suddenly that she *was* too tired to talk.

But now she wished the guide would waken. If she didn't find out what was going on and where they were, she would . . . Would what? she asked herself wryly. At this point there wasn't much she could do about anything.

She could freshen up. Maybe that would improve her outlook. She strode into the narrow bathroom, obviously once a closet, and turned on both faucets in the old-fashioned basin. After she'd splashed cold water on her face, she felt better.

When she cut off the water, she heard the door to the hall opening. Conscious of her scanty nightgown, she peered cautiously around the edge of the bathroom door.

The old woman, dressed the same as the night before, carried a tray to the table near the windows, put it down and slowly set out two plates, silverware, a silver jug, coffee cups, a basket topped by a napkin, and two small pots. When the tray was empty, she placed it carefully on the floor and walked into the hall, pulling shut the door. She hadn't once glanced around the room.

Nan hurried to the table. Food! She hadn't eaten anything since noon yesterday, when she and Leslie and Jack had shared four fabulous pizzas in a little café near the hotel. And now she was—she didn't know where she was! But she'd worry about that after breakfast.

She was lifting the napkin from its basket when Miss Mitchell called out, "Good morning, fellow prisoner," and swung out of bed. "I believe I'll join you."

Bending over the table, she removed the lids from the little pots. "Umm, orange marmalade and strawberry jam."

"And a dozen hard rolls," Nan reported happily. "At least they're generous with food."

"I don't imagine starving us is on the agenda, whatever that may happen to be," Miss Mitchell said while pouring the steaming coffee into the cups. Nan added a double helping of milk to hers. When the first pangs of hunger were satisfied, she asked, "And what do you think is on their agenda?"

Miss Mitchell finished her coffee. "I don't know," she admitted. "But I'm afraid it isn't as simple as it appears on the surface." She stood up, moved to her suitcases and pulled out two skirts and blouses. "Try these on for size," she instructed, tossing an outfit to Nan.

Nan caught the clothes, but she made no move to dress. "Simple!" she exclaimed. "It doesn't seem simple to me! How could it be any more complicated?"

Her companion paused as she tucked her blouse into her skirt. "Do you have any idea where we are?"

"Yugoslavia?" Nan offered uncertainly.

"Just barely, if my guess is right," Miss Mitchell replied. "The Dalmatian coast is fringed by dozens of islands. I think we're on one of them."

"And that makes it more complicated?" Nan asked.

"Yes," Miss Mitchell said, "Because there could be only one reason for the Yugoslavians to kidnap someone like me."

"Why?"

"To pretend I'm a spy, to charge me with espionage and try me, so that they could embarrass the United States," Miss Mitchell explained. "That's the simple explanation, even though it didn't occur to me last night. But it won't hold water here." She gestured around the room.

Nan looked around at the elegant furniture, the polished floor, the gracefully curtained windows. "I think I see your point. This isn't a jail. Certainly not the sort I'd expect for political prisoners."

Her companion nodded. "Right. Instead, it's a luxury villa on a remote Dalmatian island."

The sun shone brightly, but it seemed like sinister and cheerless gilding on their cage.

Miss Mitchell studied Nan's face, hesitated, then said, "And there's one more thing. The language spoken by our host and the man who caught you on the beach—it's Russian."

"Russian!" Nan exclaimed. "Are you sure?"

"Oh, yes, I'm sure," Miss Mitchell answered. "I was a language major in college."

"Russian," Nan repeated. "Then you don't believe they're Yugoslavian agents?"

"No," Miss Mitchell replied.

"Why should Russian agents kidnap us and bring us to Yugoslavia?"

"I don't know, but I'm going to stir up the hornet's nest and see if I can find out. Hurry and get your clothes on."

Nan quickly slipped out of her gown and began to dress. As she buttoned the bright yellow blouse, the woman walked to the door, stepped out of her shoes, picked one up and began to pound steadily on the frame.

It didn't take long to get results. An angry voice shouted, "Shut that up!" They heard the heavy tread of a man hurrying up the stairs. The key rasped in the lock. The prisoners stepped back as the door was flung open.

"What's all this?" Steven demanded, his beefy, red face tight with fury.

"We want to see your boss," Miss Mitchell said calmly.

"What you want couldn't matter less," the big man snarled.

"You might tell him," she continued, "that it's very interesting to hear Russian spoken as well as he speaks it. And, by the way, where did you study Russian?"

The man stopped still, his shoulders hunched in shock. He stared at the young woman. "You should've kept your mouth shut," he said slowly. He hurried out without another word, slamming and locking the door behind him.

"That should shake them up a little," the guide announced with satisfaction.

Nan studied her friend's face. She wasn't sure whether Miss Mitchell was brave or foolhardy, but she certainly had iron nerves.

"Let's wait in comfort," Miss Mitchell suggested. She crossed the room and pulled two overstuffed chairs close to the windows. They were sitting there, apparently relaxed, when the leader came into the room.

"I'm told you understand Russian," he began.

Miss Mitchell nodded. "Quite well," she replied.

"So you realize we are not Yugoslavians," the man continued in his high precise voice.

"Exactly. And I wonder where that leaves us?"

The man's face flattened as a snake's before it strikes. She'd pushed him too far, Nan thought. In the tense silence, the room seemed to grow and every detail was as clear and distinct as the fat black letters on an eye chart—a water stain that angled beneath the far window, the spider edging slowly across the dusty valance on the four-poster bed, the dark mole that disfigured the Russian's neck. And then the tension lessened. His thin, bloodless lips stretched in a grim smile.

"So you've discovered our little secret," he said reflectively. "Of course, if we'd taken Dr. Yates as we had planned, no word of Russian would have been uttered and he would have thought he was being kidnapped by the Yugoslavians. A Slavic *AS* airs expert such as he would speak the language. But I must admit it didn't occur to me that you understood Russian, my bright Miss Mitchell. Ah well, that'll only make your situation more amusing." And his high whinnying laugh filled the room.

"Apparently you've been very clever," Miss Mitchell said mockingly. "Perhaps you'd like to share the joke since we're in no position to pass it on."

The man cocked his head and pursed his mouth, then nodded smugly. "It will do no harm," he conceded. "And we have been rather clever. We intend to create a crisis in the relations between the United States and Yugoslavia. You, Miss Mitchell, will be our instrument. The Yugoslavians will catch you committing a very serious act of espionage.

"As I said, we first selected your compatriot, Dr. Yates, to play the role. But every time we tried to kidnap him, something went wrong—not that our intelligence has been haphazard," he added quickly. "Our agent on the spot has been close to your tour group ever since it sailed from New York. As a matter of face, she discovered you were a CIA agent before you ever set foot in France. When it became apparent that the professor was always surrounded by young people, our agent made a very intelligent suggestion. She thought we should kidnap you, and you'll do very well indeed."

"But that's impossible," Nan protested. "You can't *make* Miss Mitchell spy on the Yugoslavians."

The man chided her, "All things are possible, young lady, with the proper preparation. There's a traitor highly placed in the Ministry of Defense, and for some time now, he's been giving us most interesting information."

"But where does Miss Mitchell fit into this?"

"Very simple," he laughed. "One of our agents who resembles Miss Mitchell will use your altered passport to enter Yugoslavia. She'll meet the ministry spy in Belgrade, receive the information and hide it. Then we'll anonymously inform the police that certain secrets have been passed to an American woman. We set Miss Mitchell loose in Belgrade, the police find her very easily, and the game is over." He sighed regretfully. "Of course, this will cause us to lose the services of the man in the ministry, but our gain will far outweigh the loss."

"He won't protect you," Miss Mitchell said, "when he realizes he's been double-crossed. He'll tell everything he knows."

"What he 'knows' can only help us," the Russian retorted.

"The original contact with him was made by one of our agents who happens to be an American. You see, he thinks he's been working for the Americans all along." The man laughed. "Frightfully clever, don't you think?"

Nan closed her eyes. It was horrible.

Miss Mitchell insisted, "It still won't work. The U.S. will know I'm not a spy. And why shouldn't I repeat what you've just said when I'm picked up by the Belgrade police?"

"I don't believe you'll do that," the man responded arrogantly. "No, as soon as Miss Russell's passport is altered, an agent resembling you will cross the border and our plan goes into operation. You won't do anything to stop it."

"I certainly won't cooperate."

The man turned slowly toward Nan. The bony face with its deep eyes and beaked nose reminded her of a bird of prey. He said nothing. He looked steadily at the girl.

Miss Mitchell's face thinned. "I see," she said dully. "If I speak, then Nan. . . ." And her voice trailed off.

"Precisely," the Russian replied.

17

FOUR FEET TO FREEDOM

The captives sat for a moment in silence after the Russian and his agent left. Nan stared hopelessly at the closed door. Finally she rose from her chair and walked to the table for the silver jug. She asked, "Will you have some more coffee, Miss Mitchell?"

"Yes, thanks. But for heaven's sake, call me Karen. We're a little beyond formalities."

Nan almost managed a smile. She carried the cups across the room and handed one to her companion. "What are we going to do, Karen?"

"I don't know."

Nan clutched her cup in both hands. She could feel the warmth of the liquid spreading through her. Life went on in all the little ways. The sun shone as brilliantly here as in Kansas. The sweet scent of honeysuckle echoed a thousand other summer days. But nothing was the same or ever could be again.

Though she accepted this, her mind protested. "It can't work!" she insisted. "It can't!"

"I'm afraid it can, my dear," Miss Mitchell answered quietly as she sipped her coffee. "The evidence will be pretty clinching as far as the Yugoslavians are concerned—missing information, a traitor who thinks he's working for the U.S., a suspect—me—who fits the description of his contact. No, it can work."

Nan swallowed some coffee. "If you tell the Yugoslavians about the Russian and Steven. . . ."

"No," Miss Mitchell said. "I won't do that. Anyway, it wouldn't do any good. They won't believe a word I say when they discover I work for the CIA."

"That's really their master stroke," Nan agreed.

"Yes," Miss Mitchell replied. "And I wonder whom we have to thank for that?" She hesitated, then asked, "Did you tell anyone on the ship that you suspected me?"

Nan shook her head. "No, and I didn't tell Leslie and Jack until Paris."

"Someone discovered my identity on the ship. Miss Jones, that was the name he said. Who could it have been?"

"She must've been at the hotel yesterday, too, and seen me leave the note. And she was the one who told Steven to bring me here."

"Let me think," her companion said. "That means she knows you, Nan."

Nan was puzzled. "Someone who knows me and who discovered your identity on the ship," she repeated. "I wonder—if you were a Russian agent and the bags of your cabinmate were searched, what would you think?"

Miss Mitchell's eyes narrowed and she smiled. "I'd think the searcher had made a mistake, that someone meant to rifle through my luggage—and I'd be very anxious to know who'd done it." She considered for a moment. "That must have been the tip-off. And you said earlier that one of your cabinmates had even seen me enter the stateroom."

Nan nodded.

"All right," Miss Mitchell continued briskly. "Tell me everything you can remember about your shipmates."

Nan described Mrs. Royston with her fluffy white hair and incessant chatter, and Miss Dawes with her finely-bred face and casual self-assurance.

"A teacher from Conway, Montana, and an antique dealer from Rochester, New York," Miss Mitchell repeated. "Which one?"

"It seems impossible that it was either of them," Nan said.

"One of them is wearing a mask," Miss Mitchell insisted, "and we're going to rip it away."

Nan stared at her in astonishment. "How do you suggest we manage that?"

"I don't have an idea right now," Miss Mitchell said, "but don't think we're going to let them get away with their precious plot."

"There's no way in the world we can stop it—or Miss Jones," Nan said defeatedly.

"Oh yes, there is."

"How?" Nan asked.

"Escape," Miss Mitchell replied, her green eyes shining like a cat's.

"Escape! We might as well wish for the Marines!"

"Stop acting like a heroine tied to the rails," Miss Mitchell said. "We're a long way from that point yet. They can't put their plan into effect until your passport is altered. And that should give us at least until tomorrow."

Nan flushed. She almost got angry and then she paused. Karen was right. It wouldn't help to turn up her toes and say 'die' before they even tried.

"All right," she said. "I'm game but how do we do it, Houdini?"

"We start by exploring every inch of this room. Maybe there's a secret passage. We can always dream."

It was a short search. The walls harbored no secrets. No convenient trap door nestled in the closet. The bathroom was just a bathroom. They turned their attention to the massive wooden door that barred them from the hall.

"I don't suppose you know how to jimmy a lock, whatever that means?" Nan asked.

Miss Mitchell shook her head. "I'm afraid that's not one of my talents." She studied the door. "Even if we had an axe, it wouldn't faze that monster." Turning back toward the room, she gazed at the ornate furniture, the immense bed, the chairs and table.

"That leaves the windows," she said finally and walked toward them.

The windows—and that sheer drop to the jagged rocks below, Nan thought. As she watched, the young woman leaned far over the sill, balancing precariously on her stomach. Nan closed her eyes. When she heard no sound, she tentatively opened them. Miss Mitchell was not only still hanging out the window, she was tipped over the sill. Only the tight grip of her right hand kept her steady. Nan breathed an audible sigh of relief when her companion's head came back into view and her legs thumped onto the floor. She remained by the open frame, looking soberly down. "If we only had a rope," she began tentatively.

"We don't," Nan interrupted, "and even with a rope, it's—" she stopped and swallowed, "—it's a terribly long way down."

"Yes," Miss Mitchell agreed. "But there's a little stretch of rock before the drop. Has to be, of course. Nobody builds anything teetering on the edge of a cliff. Not enough leeway for us to jump, though."

Nan didn't even bother to answer that one. She would rather

waste away on this island for years than attempt a fifteen-foot jump with nothing but a couple of feet between her and the rim of a cliff.

Miss Mitchell nodded to herself. "Well, that's all there's to it. We'll make us a rope."

"Can you make rabbits appear too and colored handkerchiefs with goldfish?" Nan asked.

The young woman grinned. "I'll try those another time. No, it's the oldest joke in all the cartoons. But we're going to find out if it works." She paused, then continued, "And, one way or another, we're going to make it work. Come on."

Miss Mitchell strode to the bed, pulled away the rumpled quilt and began to strip off the sheets. Nan watched dubiously. "You aren't trying to tell me that we're really going to tear those into strips and knot them together and then try to climb down?"

"We're going to do a little better than that," Miss Mitchell said. "Have you ever thought much about a rope? Part of its strength is from intertwining the strands. So we're going to cut out our strips and twist them tightly together. And I'll bet we come up with a pretty good rope."

"It'll have to be very good before I'll try it," Nan said, but she helped remove the sheets and put the quilt back in place.

They carried the two big sheets into the bathroom, along with Miss Mitchell's manicure scissors, and set to work. The thick, unbleached muslin was sturdy.

"It might work," Nan admitted.

Miss Mitchell's eyes glinted with excitement and she hummed a little tune as she carefully nicked the top of the sheet at two-inch intervals.

"That'll give us about fifty strands," she announced. With only one pair of small scissors, it was hard work. Nan held the cloth steady while Miss Mitchell cut. With the bathroom door closed, it soon became hot and stuffy. It was almost eleven o'clock when they finished the first sheet.

Nan looked at the second sheet. Even Miss Mitchell was daunted. "Let's go ahead and see what we can do with these strips," she suggested. "We've got to get out before sundown—and it will take us hours just to cut the other sheet."

Nan picked up two of the strips from her pile and stared at them. "Should we tie them at the tip end before we start braiding?"

Her companion looked dubious. "I suppose so. They have to hold together somehow."

They knotted the ends of the two strips together, and Nan held the knot while Miss Mitchell tightly twined the lengths round and round. They were so absorbed in keeping the line taut that the opening of the door from the hall didn't register until they heard the steady plod of footsteps in their room.

Miss Mitchell frantically stuffed the strips beneath the raised bathtub while Nan dropped the uncut sheet over the pile of strips, plopped down on her back and began to lift her legs up and down in a muscle-tightening exercise. Her companion turned on both faucets and began to scrub her face.

When a knock sounded on the door, Miss Mitchell looked around one last time before opening it.

"Yes," she said, flinging the door wide.

The old woman stood there, merely glancing at Nan, who hoped she'd hurry. It was a tough exercise, but she continued to raise and lower her legs, counting aloud, "One and two and three and . . ."

The servant gestured toward the table, muttered something incomprehensible, bowed, and left. When the hall door had closed firmly behind her, Miss Mitchell began to laugh. She clasped her cheeks with her hands, but she couldn't stop. "You can stop now," she choked, "she just wanted to tell us lunch was here."

Nan began to giggle. She laughed until her sides ached. "Crazy Americans," she sputtered. Finally she pulled herself weakly up. All that effort to hide their pitiful scraps from detection was wasted on an old woman who was probably convinced that they were just slightly crazy.

"We are a little hysterical," Miss Mitchell declared. "And as the woman said, it's lunchtime." But she took no chances that anyone might discover their handiwork. The scraps were hidden beneath the bed, well out of view.

After a solid lunch of roast beef, green beans, a salad and strawberries, they set to work in earnest. As the afternoon dragged by, Nan felt she would scream if she had to plait just one more strand. But she kept at it.

"It's taking forever," she moaned when they stopped briefly about three o'clock to rest their weary hands and wrists.

"We'll make it," Miss Mitchell answered firmly.

When they finished, the sun was a reddish-orange fireball on the horizon. Each of the three segments of the rope contained sixteen strands, tightly interwoven. When the three thick lengths were knotted end-to-end, they had about fifteen feet of sturdy line.

"Do you know," Nan said, tired but surprised, "I think we can make it."

Miss Mitchell nodded. "We've got a good chance."

This time they were on the alert for the old woman's arrival and the rope was well-hidden before the door was unlocked. They hurried through dinner.

"Her cooking is almost too good to treat so casually," Miss Mitchell remarked, but she didn't slow down.

Nan agreed, but her mind wasn't on the meal or the rope. She was picturing the sheer, sharp drop beneath their windows. She put down her fork and took a deep gulp of water. All afternoon she'd concentrated on making the rope. She'd avoided facing its purpose.

She couldn't do it.

Nan looked up, ready to speak, when she saw her companion's abstracted look. Miss Mitchell was gently rubbing her left forearm and wrist.

"Your arm. I forgot about your arm! Can you climb with it?"

Miss Mitchell glanced at her with startled eyes. "I don't know, my dear," she admitted.

Nan pushed back her plate. "There can't be any question about it. We've got to find out if that wrist can take the strain." She looked around the room.

"Okay," Nan said, "here's how we'll do it." She dragged a straight chair to the open bathroom door. "Stand on the chair and grab the top of the frame. I'll take the chair away and you hang there."

Slowly Miss Mitchell obeyed. Climbing onto the seat, she grasped the top of the door and held tight. Nan pulled the chair away. "All right. Try holding with just your left hand."

Miss Mitchell didn't respond.

"You've got to," Nan insisted, "because that's the way you'll go down that rope—one hand after the other."

Miss Mitchell reluctantly loosened her right hand. In only an instant, she gasped with pain and her left hand slipped. She fell to the floor.

"Are you hurt?" Nan cried.

"No. But you're right. It's no go." She gazed disgustedly at her injured arm. "Why did it have to happen? I can't do it."

"I'd say it's better to know now than—" And the girl pointed toward the open windows.

"There is that," Miss Mitchell agreed with a spark of grim humor. She pulled herself up and began to pace slowly around the room.

"We have to get out of here," she said. "We *have* to! It isn't just us. There's so much at stake. More than we even realize. We can't let them get away with it."

Nan moved toward the windows and looked out at the drop. If she slipped, she'd be a crumpled heap on those sharp-edged rocks. The sea would crash in and . . . She fought away a sudden wave of nausea. But Miss Mitchell's words echoed and re-echoed within her. So much at stake. . . .

She rested her head against the cool wood of the window frame and closed her eyes. It was up to her.

She opened them and stared out at the sea, glowing in the sunset.

"Bring the rope here," she said huskily.

Miss Mitchell looked puzzled, but drew the makeshift line from beneath the bed.

"Let's see where we can tie it," Nan continued. "If I can make it down, I'll get you. The key hangs right by the door—at least, it did last night."

"It won't be easy," Miss Mitchell warned. "I thought we'd have a chance if we could get out and head straight for the motorboat. But if you try to creep back into the house, they'll catch you for sure."

Nan shrugged. "We won't be any worse off than we are now. And we've got to try."

"Can you steer a motorboat?" her companion asked suddenly.

Nan shook her head.

"Oh," Miss Mitchell sighed. "If you could—"

"I'm not going without you," Nan answered. "Come on, we're wasting time. Let's get this line hooked up."

It sounded simple. Hook up the line.

The windows were quite ordinary, made of wood with no protrusions. Where could they tie the rope?

Miss Mitchell looked around the room, and then she smiled. "Let's move that big chest closer. We can put the line around one of the legs."

The massive chest stood about six feet away from the windows. Miss Mitchell grasped one end and Nan the other. They strained to move it. The chest didn't budge. They tried again, but the immense piece of furniture slid only an inch across the floor.

"We can't do it." Miss Mitchell panted. "It would be perfect. It's certainly heavy enough to take your weight, but it's too far from the windows."

Nan frowned. "It'll take a couple of feet of line to knot it to the chest, then another six or seven feet to reach over the sill. That would leave me six feet out the window."

"And this story is fifteen feet high at least," Miss Mitchell said. She shook her head. "It's too chancy. You'd have to jump straight down with a sheer drop behind you and only a narrow ledge to land on."

"No," Nan interrupted impatiently. "It's not that bad. I'm five feet three. If I got to the end of the rope, I'd only have to drop about four feet."

"Don't try to make it sound easy," her friend cautioned. "It would be like jumping backward off a bridge with a two-foot piece of board to land on and a forty-foot fall if you stumbled."

"If I don't think about it, I'm sure I can do it. It's easy. Four feet. That's all there's to it. Four feet between us and freedom." She grabbed one end of the rope and slipped it around the thick, solid leg of the chest.

"Come on," she continued. "We don't have time to try

anything else. They may come at any moment to whisk you off to Belgrade."

When the line dangled out the window, Nan stood for a long moment, her hands tightly gripping the sill. She looked at the pearl-gray sea and the sinking sun. A brisk breeze rustled the green pines and graceful palms.

The longer she hesitated, the harder it would be.

She touched Miss Mitchell's arm and said, "I'll be back."

18

"THAT DOES IT!"

Holding tightly to the sill, Nan eased backward out the window. When she hung full-length, she took a deep breath and slowly started down.

"Don't think," she commanded herself. "Do not think. One hand after another. That's all there is to it."

Talking to herself, she tried to smother the fear that almost overwhelmed her. She fought the desire to look down. Her arms began to ache. They felt as if they'd tear from their sockets.

If she'd known about this before, she would have gone on a diet. Don't panic, she warned herself. Just take it easy—one hand after another. How much farther?

Her right hand slid down and met nothing. There was no rope left. This was it.

"Straight down," she said aloud. "Pretend you're jumping off the front porch at home."

Her arms tensed and then she paused. It'd be better if she

turned around and jumped facing the drop. But if she saw that sheer drop . . . All right she'd look. She'd made it this far.

Carefully she turned and pressed her back to the wall. Far beneath her, the sea surged in relentlessly. The waves dashed into the rocks, foaming and swirling. The rim of the cliff was no more than two feet from the villa.

Nan fastened her eyes on the narrow strip of rocky ground, breathed a prayer and let go. She landed squarely on the edge. For one sweet moment the sudden shock was the feel of success. And then the soles of her shoes slid on the loose rocks. She swayed wildly, trying to regain her footing, but it was no good.

As she began to fall, she arched her back and turned, clawing the air. Her elbow smashed against the side of the cliff, her hands scrabbled frantically for a hold. A scrawny bush about two feet beneath the lip of the drop broke her fall. She grasped its thorny branches. It sagged, but held firm to its crevice in the wall and she hung there, quivering and sick. She could hear the water beneath, sucking and hissing as it sliced past the rocks.

Her arms ached for relief. Slowly she pulled herself up, until her chest was even with her hands. Her whole being was concentrated on the sixteen inches of cliff face to the top. She mustered every last ounce of strength, thrust her right hand up to the edge of the cliff and clamped her fingers around it. Using that tiny bit of leverage, she arched her fingers like iron claws and inched her hand forward.

She found a tiny fissure in the ledge and dug her scratched and bleeding fingers into it. Desperately she loosened her grasp on the bush and swung her left hand over the rim and into the little groove.

Her hold was no more than a fingertip deep. Cautiously she lodged her knee in the angle between the bush and the cliff, pressing hard against the rock to maintain her precarious balance. With the double support she inched her chest over the rim, clutching a protruding rock. She was safe.

Numbly she crawled to the side of the building and huddled against it, trembling and exhausted. Her heartbeat gradually slowed and her breath ceased to shudder. She heard Miss Mitchell calling, but she was too tired to answer.

Nan patted the gritty surface of the rock. Her hand stung, but she savored the touch of the tiny, sharp rock prickles. She took a deep breath of the rosemary-scented air. The sky was dusky now, with only a few swaths of rose streaking the horizon. She watched the darkening water. Every ebb and surge seemed marked with sinuous grace.

It didn't matter how much she ached or how frightened she'd been. It was enough to be alive and to see twilight settling on the water.

But it wasn't quite enough. She couldn't ignore the cautious, worried cry above. Slowly she rose, leaned against the wall of the villa and looked up.

"Nan, answer me!" Miss Mitchell called softly. "Are you all right?"

"Yes," she whispered hoarsely. "Everything's fine. I'll get the key."

"Do you think you can manage?"

Nan rested for a half-second more, then stood straight and replied firmly, to her own surprise, "It'll be duck soup. Just wait and see."

She moved a little unsteadily on the rim of the cliff, her goal—the heavy wooden door through which they'd entered the past night. She paused midway up the path. She couldn't just march right in the back door—she'd better try the windows. Turning back, she hurried to the corner of the building. She peered cautiously around. By day, the pomegranates would glow a deep fiery red and the scarlet bougainvillaea could be as bright as a cardinal. In the soft dusk, their colors were muted but still vibrant. No human intruded on the peace of the scene.

Quietly she slipped around the corner and approached an open French window—the study where the hawk-nosed Russian had received them. Only the scuffing sound of her shoes broke the silence. Scarcely daring to breathe, she flattened against the casement and inched her head forward until she could see into the room. It lay dark and empty.

She stepped inside and moved swiftly over the thick rug toward the door. She hesitated when she was even with the desk. She had to hurry, but she paused to open the right-hand drawer. Stapler, pens, stationery. She pushed it shut and drew out the second drawer. It was double-depth, filled with Manila folders. Nan shrugged and grabbed the first three. They were thick and bulky and just about what she could manage without awkwardness.

A wry smile barely touched her lips as she slipped them under her arm and walked quickly to the door. She was sure it wasn't the standard operating procedure of well-trained spies, but even if her hit-and-miss grab didn't provide much in the way of interesting information, it would louse up the Russian's filing system. And she owed him a little lousing up, she thought grimly.

She grasped the heavy brass doorknob and turned it as slowly and carefully as a surgeon. She could hear the muffled rattle of dishes. The kitchen must be at the other end of the wide hall, past the back door which opened into the center of the villa. She pulled the door back until she could see the passageway. Empty.

She slipped through, closed the door behind her, and turned to the stairs. Sliding next to the wall, she climbed noiselessly. The second floor hall was deserted except for deepening shadows.

Duck soup, she thought.

At first, she didn't see the black key in the gloom. Shifting the folders to her left arm, she frantically swept her right hand over the hook. There it was! The empty feeling seeped away. She unhooked it and held it tightly—a little sliver of metal that made all the difference.

Thrusting it into the keyhole, she twisted firmly to the right and the lock clicked. She pushed the door open and stepped in.

"Come on," she called softly.

"Nan!" Miss Mitchell breathed with relief. "It was so terrible when you fell—"

"Later, alligator," Nan whispered, lighthearted now with success. "Let's get out of here. Wait." She held out the folders. "Put these in one of your suitcases and bring it along. A little trifle I took from our happy Russian's desk."

"Good girl," Miss Mitchell said warmly.

In an instant the files were packed away. They stepped out into the hall, and Nan locked the door and replaced the key.

Suddenly Miss Mitchell clamped her fingers on the girl's arm. Nan heard the footsteps at the same moment. Someone was coming up the curved stairs!

Nan gestured in the opposite direction and they sped silently up the passageway, hunting for cover. The footsteps were nearing the top when Nan tried a small door at the end of the hall. It swung inward and they pushed through. They stood, the suitcase wedged between them, at the top of a narrow staircase.

Light filtered dimly through a grimy skylight.

They tiptoed down the stairs and at the base saw another closed door. Faint sounds of running water filtered through. Someone moved slowly about.

"I'll bet it leads into the kitchen," Nan whispered.

"The old woman cleaning up after dinner," her companion replied.

"We're boxed up."

"We've got to get out of here before anyone discovers we're missing," Miss Mitchell said tensely. "Let's take a look."

She edged the door open. It was the kitchen all right. A massive old range sat to the left, and straight ahead was a door, propped open to let in the cool evening air. Across the room, the old servant worked with her back to them, washing dishes in a galvanized iron sink. She paused to lift a steaming kettle and pour boiling water over the soapy crockery. She waited a moment for it to cool, then moved the dishes unhurriedly from the sink to a wide wooden drainboard. Returning to her wash water, she dipped in a roasting pan and began to scrub.

Miss Mitchell drew the door shut and whispered hastily, "Did you see? That other door must lead out to the rose garden. The old woman's a slow worker. She'll be cleaning that roaster for at least another few minutes. Let's try to creep past behind her."

"But she's sure just to feel someone near," Nan protested.

"It's a risk, but we have to take it. Daylight is almost gone and I've got to be able to see the motorboat controls."

"Okay," Nan said. "Lead on."

Miss Mitchell picked up the suitcase and reopened the door. The old woman, her heavy shoulders hunched, scoured methodically.

The guide drew off her shoes and Nan followed suit. Miss Mitchell slipped across the room, moving as lightly as a cat on muddy ground. Nan held her breath, but the old woman continued to wash, her arm moving slowly and rhythmically.

Nan suddenly felt sure that the dishwasher's thoughts weren't in the steaming kitchen at all. Perhaps as she toiled in the hot evening, she was remembering other days and other places, when she was young and the night promised more than scalding water and grease-stained pots and pans.

Easing through the door, the girl skimmed across the room. She didn't look to see whether the old woman turned. Once in the garden, she stepped into her shoes and hurried after her companion down the barely visible path. The pine trees loomed ahead, offering a hiding place. She caught up with the guide and felt almost lighthearted. Success was within their grasp.

"Not far now," Miss Mitchell whispered, when the path curved among the evergreens.

They jogged along, sure of escape.

Miss Mitchell stopped abruptly, then pulled Nan down to the ground behind a scratchy pine. She pointed ahead.

Nan peered through the deepening twilight. It was almost funny in a horrible sort of way. The man who'd climbed the stairs might have caught them, or the old servant in the kitchen. But, no, they'd passed those hurdles—and it didn't seem fair that a fisherman should bar the way.

But he did. Halfway down the pier, a husky man leaned contentedly against the top of a piling. Pulling a fish from his line, he leisurely began to re-bait the hook. His pipe glowed in the darkness.

"That does it," Nan moaned. "He'll be there forever!"

19

ACROSS THE ADRIATIC

Her companion didn't answer. Nan sighed and rested her face on the carpeting of prickly pine needles. Tears ached behind her eyes, but she wouldn't let herself cry.

Miss Mitchell bent near. "Can you swim?" she asked.

Nan looked up hopefully and nodded.

Miss Mitchell gestured toward the beach. "The pine trees will give cover all the way to the pier, then we can crawl behind those boulders to the water and swim to the boat. But it's about seventy yards out and that's a long way. Are you really good?"

"Don't worry," Nan replied. "I'll make it. I'm a product of ten years' instruction at the Y."

Miss Mitchell looked unhappy. "The ocean isn't much like a pool."

"No," Nan admitted, "but a good swimmer is a good swimmer." And then she asked with concern, "How about you? Can you manage with your arm?"

Miss Mitchell laughed softly. "I'm part seal, darling. Let's try it." She paused. "The suitcase. We can't manage it. We'll have to leave it behind."

Nan held back. "Wait a minute," she insisted, snapping open the case. She rummaged through the clothes and lifted out a light cotton bathrobe. Wrapping it tightly around the Manila folders, she tied her package with the robe's sash, leaving the ends dangling. "Now fasten it to my shoulder," she said.

Miss Mitchell strapped the bundle on her back. They crawled toward the beach and then she rose to a crouch and followed her companion across the sand into the cold water. Her scratched hands burned in the salty water as they made their way through the waves.

"Watch the next breaker," Miss Mitchell warned suddenly. "It's a big one." The wave towered above them, beginning to foam at the crest. "Dive through!" Miss Mitchell cried.

Nan cut through the wall of water. The bundle lurched but the fastening held. She shuddered at the shock of cold, but as she began to swim at a steady crawl, excitement tingled through her. Even with the awkward lump of soggy papers on her back, she felt free and safe, exhilarated by the water. She paused once to locate her companion. Miss Mitchell was about ten feet ahead. Nan surged forward, and she was close behind when Miss Mitchell reached the boat.

"It's a beauty," Miss Mitchell murmured. "At least a twenty-three footer."

Lunging out of the water, Miss Mitchell caught hold of the low railing on the gunwale. She pulled herself aboard, steadied the boat, then turned to help Nan over the side.

"Crouch low so no one will see you," Miss Mitchell said as she turned and crept to the cockpit. She squinted at the control panel in the last vestiges of twilight, then cast off the lines.

Sliding behind the wheel, she motioned Nan forward. "Settle in," she directed, pointing to the seat on the port side.

Nan perched on the edge of the slick vinyl seat and tugged on the cord holding the files. She eased the soggy mass into her lap and leaned back. The papers would dry and perhaps they'd prove to be the downfall of the Russian agent.

The cool breeze plastered her wet clothing against her body, but she was too tense to feel the cold. She turned to watch Miss Mitchell.

"Clear the bilge," Miss Mitchell was muttering to herself. "Check the warm-up throttle. Put the control lever in neutral."

Miss Mitchell switched on the ignition key. The engine roared to life. She swung the boat to port, away from the pier. The engine died.

"Blast," she moaned. "The throttle."

In the sudden silence, Nan could hear the fisherman running down the pier. She squirmed around in her seat as Miss Mitchell worked frantically with the controls. Shouting, the man came nearer. He raced alongside as the engine purred to life, then poised for an instant, a heavy figure towering above them. Nan reached down, yanked a cushion from the seat behind and flung it in his face as he jumped for the craft. It caught him midway in his leap. Arms flailing, he fell back into the water as the motorboat leapt ahead.

Nan leaned over the back seat and strained to see him. She spotted him swimming steadily for the beach.

Turning, she settled limply in her seat, her arms and legs trembling. In the dim light from the instrument panel, she studied her companion. Her hands were relaxed on the steering wheel, and she was smiling slightly. She was enjoying herself!

The craft continued to pick up speed until it seemed to Nan they might as well be flying. Her hands tensed on the wet files.

She shouted to make herself heard over the engine's roar. "How fast are we going?"

"Top speed," Miss Mitchell replied gleefully. "About forty-five miles an hour. And that's traveling!"

"I believe it," Nan agreed. As they sped swiftly through the night, the craft skimming over the water almost without a jolt, she began to relax. This was fun! And they had made it. They were free. It was not until safety was almost within their grasp that she'd admitted to herself how terrifying it all had been. Prisoners of Russian spies!

She tried to wrench her mind away from the terrors that still seemed so near. Could they be following? But in the heavy black of the night, she saw no light, no movement.

"How do you know which way to go?" she asked, suddenly only too aware of the emptiness of the sea.

Miss Mitchell tapped a small spherical hump on the control panel. "That, my dear," she answered, "is a compass. They're optional on speedboats, but I imagine this craft is no stranger to crossing the Adriatic. Not only does it have a compass, it has two extra fuel tanks, which gives us about sixty gallons in all. And that's enough for a round trip."

"If nobody minds," Nan said, "one way's good enough for me."

She shivered from her wet clothes and the cutting wind. "How long will it take us?"

Her companion shrugged. "I'm not sure where we started from, but it's probably about a hundred or a hundred and ten miles. So we should hit the Italian coast in a couple of hours."

Nan settled back in her seat and shrunk into a tight ball. What she would give for a wool blanket and some hot, hot coffee! She gave up trying to talk over the loud throb of the motor and the whoosh of the wind.

She didn't know how much time had passed when she started

to hear a different sound. Something must be wrong! And then she knew. That roar, that steady zoom wasn't from their engine. It was a plane!

Miss Mitchell said crisply, "It's flying low to the water. Over there—to the southwest. Seems to be looking for something. Care to guess who?"

The old familiar sick feeling of fear surged through the girl. The seaplane! She hadn't even thought about the seaplane.

"Will they see us?" she asked.

"No," Miss Mitchell answered. "That's why, Miss Landlubber, we don't have our running lights on. It's highly illegal, but that's the least of our worries at the moment. I didn't think they'd let us go without a struggle, but the chase has just begun."

"Just begun?" Nan repeated.

Miss Mitchell glanced at her quickly. "Yes," she continued lightly. "We aren't exactly going to wade triumphantly ashore, shouting 'Here we are.' As our recent hosts see it, we've got to be stopped. They know pretty well where we'll land, so I imagine every available fellow-traveler in Italy will be out looking for two rather untidy American girls."

"I see," Nan said quietly. "What are we going to do?"

"Punt," Miss Mitchell said. "No, really, don't worry," she continued in a more sober tone. "We'll figure out a way. We've made it this far, haven't we?"

This far, Nan thought. This far and how much farther?

The sound of the plane faded in the distance. Miss Mitchell hunched over the steering wheel, pulling every last particle of speed from the motor. "We should be nearing land soon."

Nan peered through the night. As the minutes crawled by, her eyes began to tire. No lights anywhere on the horizon. The pale new moon illuminated only the dark water.

But suddenly she strained to hear. Could it be? She leaned across and yelled, "Can we stop for a minute?"

Miss Mitchell looked at her in surprise, but she slowed the craft. As the sound of the motor softened, they both heard it—the dull roar of surf crashing to shore.

Miss Mitchell smoothly swung the boat to starboard and began to run parallel to the coast. "That was good work," she said. "We're pretty close—too close to be heading in at full speed. I think our luck must be riding high tonight."

"Why aren't there any lights?" Nan asked.

"This isn't a very heavily populated section of Italy," she explained. "And not many of the poorer people have electricity. We'll keep going until we spot some sort of village."

It was a good half-hour before they saw a small cluster of lights in the hills above the coastline.

"I think we'll take it, whatever it is," the guide said. She slowed the craft until the engine ran at a soft whisper. In the thin light of the moon, they could barely make out several small piers in an inlet. Six or seven single-masted vessels moved sluggishly at their moorings. "A fishing village," Miss Mitchell said. She cut the motor and the boat began to drift. "Do you feel up to another swim?"

"Swim?" Nan repeated. "Why?"

"No matter how quietly we'd slip into a pier, someone might hear the engine. And that someone might be quite prepared to haul us back to that lovely villa across the way."

"You think they might have an agent here?"

"As I said," the woman replied, "landing spots are few and far between on this coast. And they've had a couple of hours to lay out a dragnet."

"I can swim it," Nan said firmly. "Help me retie the packet. It's come this far and it's going all the way."

Once the soggy mass of papers was back in place, Nan took a deep breath and said, "Let's go."

"Head for that small pier over there and try to keep in the shadow of the pilings," Miss Mitchell directed.

"Okay," Nan answered. She slipped carefully over the side, her muscles tensed against the cold. She gasped as she sank into the chill water.

She'd gone about halfway when her arms and legs began to tire. A high swell slapped her unexpectedly across the face. Choking, she floundered for a moment and a little flare of panic tightened her chest. Miss Mitchell pulled next to her, whispering, "Cramp?"

Her fear subsided as Miss Mitchell's voice reached her. "Sorry, Karen," she murmured. "Just a little tired. I'm all right now." She struck off again, moving heavily, one stroke at a time. That was all she had to do. One stroke at a time.

Concentrating on lifting one arm after the other, she passed the point where the breakers began, sensing that the trough would be deep, and she'd have to fight against the backsweep.

"Nan!" Miss Mitchell screamed. "The breaker! Dive back, dive back."

Nan twisted her head and saw the huge mass of water poised to crash. Frantically, she pulled around to try and dive beneath it. The crest fell as she turned and the roiling water threatened to tumble her head-over-heels, but she grimly churned ahead and finally the water was calm again. Her companion drew close. "Hold on, there's another one coming. Face the beach and when I give the word, swim fast. We can catch the crest and ride it in. Just put your head down and point like an arrow."

As long as she didn't have to see the towering wave, she could do it, Nan thought. She kept her head facing the shore. She'd leave it up to Karen.

"Go!" Miss Mitchell called.

Nan began to stroke. She felt herself lifted by the water, up, up, and then the wave crashed and she rode the breaker, whooshing along at breakneck speed. This was terrific! When you were on the wrong side, a cresting wave was terrifying, but to fling yourself forward at the right instant and roar toward the shore was fabulous. No wonder people liked to surf! The dull exhaustion which had threatened to overwhelm her began to ebb. When the wave was spent and her knees scraped the sandy bottom, she almost regretted it. Someday she'd surf for fun, not survival.

Nan felt weak, but she followed her companion into the deep shadows of the pier with confidence. As the water surged and eddied around their knees, Miss Mitchell leaned close to whisper, "Stay right on my heels."

Nan marveled at the woman's endurance as she moved steadily ahead with no sign of weariness. Nan pushed a little harder. They crossed the beach and ran for the cover of a series of corrugated-iron shacks. No one moved in the dim moonlight. The only sound was the roar of the breakers. The little village lay asleep on the hill facing the narrow beach.

"I think I see a path. It's probably a back way into the village. Let's try it," Miss Mitchell suggested. "We might be a little less conspicuous—if anyone's looking this way."

Stumbling among sharp-pronged brambles, they trudged up a sandy hill. At the top, Miss Mitchell studied the ramshackle houses scattered below. Nan sat down in the thick weeds and rested her face on her knees. The soggy bundle of files was heavy on her back, but she didn't have enough energy to loosen them. She was so tired. When her companion tapped on her arm, it took a long moment before she looked up.

"I don't know where we'll go from here," Miss Mitchell began, her voice for the first time reflecting some strain. "It's just a tiny place."

Her words were drowned by the deep rumble of a truck crawling up a sharp grade. Miss Mitchell swung her head toward the sound. Headlights flashed against the sky as the truck curved around a roadway about eighty yards from them.

"A highway!" Miss Mitchell exclaimed. "Come on, Nan, let's get to that road. Nothing can stop us now!"

20

A SCORE TO SETTLE

Moving stealthily, the fugitives passed several flat-roofed cottages. Warily they entered the main street, a lane of hard-packed dirt with a single row of small, one-story shops, now dark and silent. At the end of the street, light filtered from a bar. An outburst of loud laughter jarred the silence of the summer night.

Keeping to the shadows, they hurried up the lane, heading for a deeply-rutted road that twisted up and out of sight, just beyond the bar. Nan breathed more easily when they were beyond the doorway.

"Faster," Miss Mitchell urged when they reached the twisting road, but the soft sand dragged at Nan's feet. It was like struggling through melted marshmallows. A shadow darted about ten yards in front of her. She gasped, then saw the squirrel. As their footfalls neared, he stopped, his tiny chest quivering. They could almost touch him before he ran for cover.

Nan plodded on, wondering if his small heart trembled

when he was frightened. She had more sympathy for threatened animals now.

The road cut sharply between a thick row of pine trees. The meager glow from the moon no longer lit the way. And then they heard the engine of a truck, straining at a high pitch. As the vehicle reached the summit of the hill, its heavy wheels grated on gravel and the roar of the motor dwindled into silence.

"It's stopping," Nan gasped.

Stumbling in their eagerness, they groped their way forward. The lane opened abruptly onto the dark asphalt of a major highway. Its warning lights blinking, the vehicle was parked alongside two other massive trailers. Light blazed from the gas and diesel pumps which fronted a small café.

"The lights I saw from the sea!" Nan cried.

"It must be a truck stop," Miss Mitchell replied. "With all that transportation, we should be able to find ourselves a lift."

"A lift where?" the girl asked.

"Rome."

"Why not the nearest town?" Nan demanded. "We could go to the police station."

"And wouldn't we cause a sensation!" the woman interrupted. "I imagine everybody in town would hear about the two Americans by morning. Our island friend would find out in no time at all."

"He knows we've escaped," Nan objected. "What difference would it make?"

"Miss Jones," her companion said softly. "We have an account to settle with her. The minute word leaks out that we've reached the authorities, she'll scramble out of Italy on the first plane to any place. She can't be sure what the Russian may have revealed about her identity. But as long as we're apparently on the loose, she'll be in Rome on the lookout because that's the logical place for us to go. The American Embassy is there and so is our tour."

Nan sighed. Would it ever be over? "I'm sorry," she said irritably, "but I think it's ridiculous. Even if we make it to Rome and she's looking for us, how can we catch her? We don't know who she is!"

"There'll be a way," Miss Mitchell replied. "And we'll find it. But right now, the problem is to get to Rome. We'll tackle one thing at a time." She paused, then added, "Nan, don't you see, we can't just crawl into a safe little nest and pretend none of this ever happened. An American connived and lied to put it over. Do you want her to walk away free and snuggle comfortably into her antique shop—or her classroom?"

Nameless, faceless, merciless Miss Jones. Nan clenched her aching hands, rubbed raw in that desperate struggle up the island cliff face, and a cold anger trickled through her. "I don't want her free," she said. "Let's go find that ride!"

They approached the roadside stop, walking well in the shadows. When they reached the graveled parking area, Miss Mitchell glanced around, then motioned for Nan to follow her. Quietly they slipped across the lighted area to crouch behind a row of oil drums beside the café.

"And now we wait," Miss Mitchell said, "and see if we can spot a truck to Rome."

The minutes dragged by. Two trucks pulled in. Miss Mitchell leaned forward to listen as the attendant chatted with the drivers.

"No luck there," she whispered. "One's going to Florence and the other to Bari."

Nan shivered in her wet clothes. The thick smell of oil and gas made her dizzy. She slumped against the smooth stucco of the café, feeling absolutely miserable, and didn't even look up as another truck rolled into the station.

As a door slammed, the attendant called out, "*Dove vai stasera, Luigi*?"

"A Roma."

Even Nan understood that. Miss Mitchell gripped her arm. "This is it!"

Peering between the cans, the fugitives watched the driver tensely. He stayed near the hood while the man checked the oil. But finally he clapped the attendant on the shoulder and walked toward the café door. The station employee wiped the windshield, pulled out the gas nozzle from the tank, then sauntered out of sight.

"Come on," Miss Mitchell said.

They squirmed from behind the big cans and ran to the battered vehicle—an old black panel truck with a curtain in the rear. In the glare of the overhead lights, Nan's back tensed as Miss Mitchell pushed aside the thick burlap covering and gave Nan a boost inside.

As she moved deeper into the van, Nan collided with something heavy hanging from the roof. Reeling off-balance, she stumbled back against Miss Mitchell. The woman grabbed and caught one of the suspended objects, but her hands slipped from its greasy surface. And then the van was a nightmare of swaying, heavy lumps rustling and shushing in the air.

"What is it?" Nan asked in an hysterical voice.

"Don't scream!" Miss Mitchell said. "I don't know what it is. Wait."

Nan pressed as close to the burlap-covered exit as she could and tried to close the thudding, bumping noise out of her mind. What could be hanging from the roof? Then she heard Miss Mitchell stifle a laugh.

"It isn't bodies after all," she cried, "except in a way. We're in a truck loaded with big hams, and they're hanging from the ceiling. Come on, help me get them still again. The driver might hear them moving when he gets back."

With a grimace of distaste, Nan helped her companion steady the swinging hams. Finally all was quiet and they settled toward the front of the van, squeezed between three immense hams.

In only a few minutes, the driver returned and the truck chugged slowly away from the station. Soon it was rattling along, lurching from side to side, as it clung to the tortuously winding road. The hams seemed to possess a life of their own, thudding and slamming against the stowaways and the sides of the van. Nan huddled in the corner, protecting her head and shoulders with an upraised arm. Numb with misery, she finally fell into a half-sleep, rousing now and then to push the greasy weights away. Later she realized that the vehicle was running straight. The hams moved but no longer jounced. She stretched out gratefully and fell into a deep sleep.

"Wake up," Miss Mitchell whispered. "We're in Rome."

"Rome," Nan murmured. The sweet, fatty smell of the meat washed over her and she remembered where she was. She sat up cautiously. "How long have we been riding?"

"About four hours. We reached the outskirts just a little while ago. Dawn's breaking and we'd better get ready to get out of here."

Slithering between the suspended slabs of meat, Nan followed her to the burlap-draped rear. Every so often, the truck slowed for a signal light, then resumed its steady pace.

"Do you have any idea where we are?" Nan whispered.

In the early morning glow, the stuccoed buildings wore a golden aura, mellow with age. The street curved to pass beneath an ancient vaulted gate. On the left stood a magnificent cathedral. The graceful columns of the portico gleamed in the rose-tinted light.

"Of course," Miss Mitchell said in delight. "It's St. John of the Lateran and I do know where we are. Listen, Nan, at the next stoplight if there's no one around, we'll jump out."

The truck seemed charmed from that point on, making every green light. Finally it began to slow, and Miss Mitchell gripped the girl's arm. As soon as the vehicle rocked to a stop, she whispered, "Go!"

Nan swung over the edge stiffly, and into the street. She froze when she spotted movement halfway up the street, but then relaxed when she saw that the pedestrian was walking away from them. As the truck disappeared down the street, Nan stared ahead in disbelief. "Is that what I think it is?" she asked, gazing wide-eyed at the crumbling, cinnamon-brown walls that curved so gracefully.

Miss Mitchell smiled. "Yes, it's the Colosseum."

In the early morning stillness, Nan could almost picture the structure as it had been so many hundreds of years ago. Gladiators had battled here to live one more day. Christian martyrs had stood firmly here in the face of wild beasts.

Miss Mitchell tugged at her arm. "I know, but we can't sightsee just yet. I'm almost afraid to tell you that the Roman Forum is just over there." She made a sweeping gesture to her right.

Nan swung around to look. Just visible in the distance were the tops of the ruins that marked the heart of ancient Rome, where golden-voiced Cicero addressed the Senate, where Caesar was assassinated, where Livy was inspired to write the monumental history of the Roman state.

"Come on," Miss Mitchell urged. "We've got to deal with the present—and then you can slip into the past. Let's find a telephone." She frowned. "Did you tuck your billfold in your pocket? Good, let's hurry then. The streets'll soon be filled with people and we look a little—well—scruffy, to say the least."

Scruffy was putting it politely, Nan thought as she followed her companion up the street. Miss Mitchell's hair straggled into her face, which was bare of lipstick and powder. Her dress hung limp and wrinkled and her shoes still squished slightly as she walked.

Nan knew her own appearance wasn't any better. Probably a little worse, considering her desperate struggle on the cliff face. She hunched her shoulders self-consciously. The movement shifted the bundle on her back and she stopped short. "Karen," she hissed. "Get this packet loose. Hurry, I must look like an idiot."

Miss Mitchell looked startled, then laughed. "But, madam, it's quite the thing this season to wear a small parcel of soggy papers on your back. The effect is *chic*."

"Aren't you clever," Nan replied. "We look bad enough already."

Miss Mitchell's quick fingers were already loosening the water-tightened knots. "Here," she said, thrusting the wet mass at Nan. "Now you can pass for a wastepaper collector."

"They've come this far," Nan said, "and they're going all the way. Perhaps they can tell us something about Miss Jones."

"Perhaps they can, at that. Hold on to them, because one way or another we're going to catch her," Miss Mitchell said.

Halfway up the next block, they found a small sidewalk café with only one patron, and he was immersed in a red leather-bound volume. The fugitives sat down on the other side, well in the shadow of the awning. After ordering coffee and rolls, Miss Mitchell asked the waiter, "*Mi scusi, ha un telefono*?"

The boy nodded and motioned toward the interior. Miss Mitchell rose and followed him. She still hadn't returned when the waiter came with their breakfast. At the sight of the hard rolls and steaming coffee, Nan realized she was ravenous. In the circumstances, she was sure Miss Mitchell wouldn't want her to wait, so she devoured three rolls, liberally coated with grape jam and gulped the strong coffee. The food helped, but she still couldn't relax. She smiled grimly to herself. To think when the summer began how frightened she'd been of the coming winter in Scotland! And now she sat tensely, wondering how they could trap an elusive American traitor.

She tried to lean back more easily in her chair. At least she was safe for the moment. She put down her cup abruptly. Her mother and father! She had to let them know she was safe, immediately. It was hard to wait patiently until Miss Mitchell slipped through the doorway and came to the table.

"My contact's on the way to pick us up," she began as she slid into her seat.

Nan clutched her arm. "Karen, I've got to let my parents know everything is all right."

Miss Mitchell looked at her with concern. "Hold on a minute, lamb. Everything isn't all right until we stop Miss Jones." She held up her hand when Nan started to interrupt. "Wait. I know how upset your parents must be, but they'll just have to bear with it an hour or so longer. I'm sure our adversaries are watching them and even if they tried, your parents couldn't hide their relief if they heard you were safe."

Nan twisted in her seat. "How could the agents be watching my parents in Ethiopia? I could send a telegram." She stopped abruptly, and the words dropped like stones. "Are Mother and Dad in Rome?"

Miss Mitchell nodded. "They arrived last night," she said softly.

Nan's face glowed. "They're here," she breathed. "Oh, Karen, I'm so glad."

"Just a little while longer and you'll be with them. I know how you feel," she broke off and waved to the waiter. "Our check, please." As Nan counted out the *lire*, Miss Mitchell rose. "Come on, we've got to go."

Puzzled, Nan followed.

"Our ride's here," Miss Mitchell explained. "See that gray Volvo with the crumpled hubcap? The driver's my contact here."

When they were at the car, Miss Mitchell glanced up and down the street, then motioned Nan into the back seat while she climbed into the front. The door closed and the car began to move.

21

TO BAIT A TRAP

The driver, a round-faced man, slouched comfortably behind the wheel, his gabardine suit bunched at the shoulders.

"We're certainly glad to have you two back," he drawled. He glanced around at Nan. The quickness of his light blue eyes surprised her. It seemed to contrast oddly with his chubby face and undistinguished clothes.

"Not half as glad as we are," Nan replied.

The man gave a quick grin. As he shifted into high and swung onto a main thoroughfare, he said, "I got the main outline over the phone. Now it's time to fill in the picture. Start with Naples. Miss Mitchell first."

The man listened intently as first Miss Mitchell, then Nan, described their kidnapping. When Nan handed him the crumpled Manila folders, he smiled in delight.

"This can't help but be valuable," he commented. "You've

both done very well." He slowed the car and turned into an alley.

Nan looked out in surprise. Absorbed in their report, she'd paid no attention to the surroundings. The narrow lane led behind a block of modern apartment houses. The CIA agent pulled the car into a parking place, explaining, "Thought we might borrow a friend's apartment for a while. A little more privacy."

The trio walked quickly through a back entrance and up shiny linoleum stairs to the third floor. He unlocked the door to a tastelessly-decorated apartment with cheap modern furniture and bright pink walls.

"Make yourselves comfortable," he said.

Nan settled on an angular zebra-striped sofa with the hardest foam rubber cushions she had ever encountered. Their host started a pot of coffee, then pulled off his suit jacket and straddled a straight chair in the middle of the room.

"It boils down to this," he said. "We don't have enough information to figure out which one of Nan's cabinmates is Miss Jones. So let's start over and take it right from the beginning. There may be some small detail that'll help us."

"Look, Mr.—" and Nan looked inquiringly into his bright blue eyes.

He said nothing for a moment, then replied evenly, "Mr. Smith will do just fine."

"Miss Jones on one side and Mr. Smith on the other," the girl said. "What originality!"

He shrugged his thick shoulders, finally answering, "I suppose you could call me Red Charlie. That's my contact name with Miss Mitchell. It'd be more colorful. I should think, however, that you would've had enough color to last you a while."

For just a moment, Nan could feel the rope between her

hands and hear again the sucking whisper of the water so far below. She shivered and said, "I've had quite enough, thanks. It just seems so pointless to go over and over it. Miss Jones is too clever for us."

"Perhaps," he agreed. "But I have the time if you do."

Nan launched into a recital of the events in Naples. Mr. Smith interrupted almost immediately. "A big shambling man?" he repeated. "Describe him, please."

"Big and heavy. He has reddish blond hair and—"

"That doesn't square with the note you left for your roommate," the agent broke in. He rummaged through a briefcase on the floor, drew out a slip of paper and handed it to her. "It really threw us for a while because the description is a dead ringer for a known Yugoslavian agent who lives in Naples. We pulled him in the first thing, but he had a foolproof alibi."

Nan was reading as he spoke. "Oh no. This even looks like my writing, but it isn't what I said at all. Someone else wrote it!"

"Miss Jones again," Miss Mitchell interjected. "That means she was right there, watching to see how the scheme worked."

"It caused us quite a bit of trouble," Mr. Smith said. "Miss Whitaker tracked down her stepfather, Rowley Latimer, as soon as she and Mr. O'Neill realized you were missing. The three of them have been on everybody's back. When they discovered we'd released this Yugoslavian agent, they decided we weren't really doing our best to help you. It's been quite a three-ring circus since you disappeared."

Nan didn't change expression, but she was cheered by a warm surge of feeling. Leslie and Jack—even if they hadn't been able to help, they had tried.

"Are Leslie and Jack in Rome with the rest of the tour?" she asked.

"They certainly are," Mr. Smith replied. "One of them's at the hotel at all times in case you try to call, while the other harasses the Embassy. Today Leslie and her stepfather are camping out in the Embassy foyer."

"That's very bright of them," Miss Mitchell said. "It's logical that Nan would try to contact them. She'd be afraid to directly approach the hotel or the Embassy. But a telephone call—"

"A telephone call," the man repeated. He turned to Nan. "Is it common knowledge that you, Leslie and Jack made a threesome? Would Miss Jones know it?"

The girl nodded.

"Then you can bet Jack's being watched at the hotel," Mr. Smith asserted. "I think I see a way to find our elusive lady. Nan will call and ask Jack to meet her. When he rushes out of the hotel, Miss Jones will know something is up."

"Why should Miss Jones herself follow?" Nan asked.

"She's the only one who can definitely recognize you," Mr. Smith explained. "She may not come alone, but she'll come. And when she tries to grab you, we've got her."

Miss Mitchell wasn't so sure. "It's too dangerous," she objected. "Miss Jones'll be desperate. As far as she's concerned, Nan must be stopped at all cost. I'll be the decoy."

"You wouldn't do at all," Mr. Smith stated flatly. "The whole thing hinges on Jack O'Neill's reaction to the phone call. And he still thinks you're a spy. We haven't told him the truth yet."

"Oh," Miss Mitchell said unhappily. "But I still don't like it."

"The Italian police are extremely cooperative," Mr. Smith said. "And very efficient. The whole area will be covered with plainclothesmen."

"You just don't want to miss the finale, Karen," Nan said lightly and forced a laugh. "But the honor is all mine."

It was shortly after noon that Mr. Smith began to dial the

number of the hotel. The trap was ready—now to bait its jaws. Nan watched as his stubby forefinger twirled the dial.

When the desk clerk answered, Nan took the receiver and asked rapidly, "Please, do you speak English? Will you ring John O'Neill's room?"

It seemed an eternity before the clerk returned to the telephone. "I'm sorry, *signorina*, there's no answer. Would you care to leave a message?"

"It's very important. Will you have him paged?"

Through the open connection, she could hear voices and the click of footsteps across the lobby. Suddenly, a loudspeaker sounded: "Mr. John O'Neill. Telephone for Mr. John O'Neill."

The receiver seemed to ooze heat as she grasped it with a wet palm. That summons would flush Miss Jones. With cold certainty, Nan knew the woman was in the hotel. But whose face was drawing into tight concentration as the voice called Jack? Was it the plump, softly-wrinkled face of Mrs. Royston? Or the aloof but charming countenance of Miss Dawes?

The boy's voice erased her fantasies. But she cut in urgently, "Jack, this is Nan and I need help."

"Nan!" he repeated, stunned. And then, strongly and clearly, she heard the note of relief. "Where are you? I'll come for you."

Nan hesitated. She hated to lie, even for a moment, but the phone might be tapped and all she said had to be convincing. When Miss Mitchell touched her arm, she drew a deep breath and said hurriedly, "They're after me. Meet me at the Trevi Fountain. Please hurry!" And she depressed the cradle-bar.

Nan stood rigidly by the telephone stand. Done. And now it was time for the fly to flutter into the web. In for a penny, in for a pound, she thought. "I'd better be on my way," she said tensely. "I'll see you—later."

"Nan—take care," Miss Mitchell urged, her face drawn with

worry. The man patted her arm, and then she was in the hall, her footsteps echoing hollowly. She walked alone down the three flights of scuffed stairs and out the rear door into the brilliant burning light of midday Rome. A cab, driven by an Italian policeman in plainclothes, pulled even with her.

Nan climbed into the back seat and sat on the edge of the hot upholstery. As the cab hurtled through the streets, she stared ahead. No one had seemed to grasp one simple fact—Miss Jones wouldn't be seeking a prisoner this time.

22

MEET MISS JONES

It was one thing, Nan realized, to escape from danger and quite another to walk deliberately into it. When the taxi rounded the corner and began to slow down, she focused her eyes with effort. Its green water glittering in the sunlight, the beautiful Trevi Fountain loomed ahead. She saw Jack standing alone at the very front of the fountain. When the taxi stopped, she pulled herself stiffly out onto the curb and moved as disjointedly as a marionette. She started toward the boy, the muscles in her back tightening, cringing away from danger.

Jack saw her and ran quickly to her side. He gripped her arm tightly. "Are you all right?" he demanded. "Why did you hang up? Who's after you?"

Nan glanced from side to side. "This is a trap. I couldn't tell you over the phone because it might've been bugged.

The kidnapping plot wasn't planned by Miss Mitchell, but by a Russian agent, a woman. And we know she is either Mrs. Royston or Miss Dawes."

At his startled look, she explained hurriedly, "Miss Mitchell's CIA, and they kidnapped her instead of Dr. Yates—anyway, the CIA thinks this agent has been watching you in the hope I would call. They think the woman is following you, hoping to find me, and when she tries something," her voice faltered "—they'll catch her. There are policemen everywhere."

"Then you're a decoy," the boy said.

Nan looked at his face and suddenly she felt safer. She'd remembered him always laughing and teasing, but there was no smile now. For the first time she became really conscious of his sturdy, determined chin and solid shoulders. He wasn't just a pleasant traveling companion. He was a rugged young man. Miss Jones might win, but Jack would give it all he had.

"What should we do now?" she asked simply.

"Act as if everything you said on the phone were true and see what happens," he said. "Our logical move would be to hurry to one of the big hotels and call the Embassy from there. And that's just what we'll do."

He guided her around the low curving wall of the fountain to a bright yellow motorscooter.

"She should certainly be able to keep us in sight," the girl commented.

"I didn't know when I rented it yesterday that I'd be running from a spy," he smiled. "It seemed like a good way to get back and forth from the Embassy. Anyway, your Miss Jones can't do much when we get going. It's funny her people didn't try to grab you in front of the fountain. Maybe the CIA is wrong and she wasn't watching me."

Nan shivered. "Let's hurry."

"Hop on," he said, straddling the scooter. She climbed on the rear and clasped him tightly around the waist as he turned on the key and stomped on the pedal. The motor rumbled and they bumped over the curb into the street.

"We'll cross over here and go to—"

Nan's scream cut through his words. "Jack, that car!"

The boy turned his head to see a dusty brown Fiat picking up speed behind them. For an instant, the scooter faltered as he looked desperately around. The avenue was deserted in the midday heat.

Abruptly, he twisted the handlebar and power surged through the scooter. It leapt ahead with a violent jerk and hurtled across the square. Nan could hear the high whine of the car close behind. People shouted and a siren screamed angrily.

She looked back. The Fiat was only a few feet behind. The hot breath of its engine blew on her. Half-blinded by the sunlight, she dimly saw two persons in the front seat. She swung her eyes forward and horror flooded through her. What was Jack doing? The scooter was heading straight for the curb! Her arms tightened about him.

The machine hit the concrete ridge with a stunning jolt. All her bones shrieked in protest. The scooter soared into the air, landing with a numbing shock on the broad sidewalk. It swayed dangerously as the boy tried to keep it upright. Nan sat as still as an animal frozen by fear. If she moved even a little, their precarious balance would be gone and the scooter would topple. She wasn't thinking of Miss Jones. Every fiber of her body was bound up in the quivering machine beneath her.

Slowly, the scooter righted and picked up speed until the buildings blurred together. Jack risked a quick backward glance and muttered numbly, "Oh no."

Nan looked behind. Only a few yards away, the Fiat lurched

over the curb in steady pursuit. And then for an instant it slowed. The passenger was struggling with the driver!

"Jack!" she cried.

The boy looked around and seized the opportunity. Slowing a little, he drove the machine back over the curb and into the street. Jack swung back toward the fountain, with the scooter leaning at a fearful angle, weaving among the police cars converging on the Fiat.

The Fiat's brakes screeched as the driver tried to follow them, but midway in its turn, it jolted to a halt, blocked by a police van and three unmarked cars. Plainclothesmen dashed out of the vehicles to surround the little brown car.

Jack turned the scooter around once again. They slowly pulled even with the van and stopped. Neither moved nor spoke for a long moment. Finally the boy swung off his seat and turned to help Nan. Still shaking, she clung to him for support, and then they were the center of an excited throng.

Mr. Smith and Miss Mitchell pushed their way through. "Are you all right?" he asked.

The girl nodded wordlessly.

The agent clapped Jack on the shoulder. "Fantastic driving, son."

"Not as fantastic as my passenger," the boy replied proudly. "She didn't panic—and one wrong move would've wrecked us."

"Miss Jones?" Nan managed to ask.

The man smiled grimly. "We've got her. And she won't be able to talk her way out of this." He paused, then added hastily, "Not that I would've let you in for this if I'd thought—"

"It's over now," Nan broke in. "Don't blame yourself. And it worked. We caught her. Miss Jones has caused us quite a bit of grief in the last—" She stopped, startled. "Can it be only three days? Yes, three days. And now, I want to meet her."

She walked toward the Fiat, and stopped beside the policeman guarding the woman, who still sat in the front seat. Nan didn't even glance at the driver. She looked only at the woman, staring into eyes as dark as her own, but filled with a hard brightness—and fear.

"I tried to stop him," the woman said quickly. "I didn't know he was going to—"

"Your second thoughts came a little late," Miss Mitchell interrupted coldly. "You didn't have any qualms about tossing me into a Yugoslavian prison or leaving Nan at the mercy of that ruthless Russian."

The woman glared at them. And then the bright brown eyes, burning with hostility, clung to Nan. "It would have worked," she said shrilly, "if you'd minded your own business."

Nan stepped back involuntarily. She looked in disbelief at the plump grandmotherly face. "Are you really a schoolteacher?" she asked. "And you have two granddaughters? One just my age?"

Mrs. Royston's eyes blinked rapidly. She began to laugh harshly, and then clutched a fleecy shawl to her face and began to cry.

23

GOOD-BYE TO ROME

Moonlight dappled Rome, softening the lines of the centuries-old buildings and bathing marble and stone with milky-light. In the soft, warm night air, the clip-clop of the horse's hooves echoed through the empty streets.

"It's late," Jack said finally, breaking a long, contented silence. "You both must be tired. Perhaps we'd better get back to the hotel. We leave early tomorrow for Florence."

"Let's not go back yet," Leslie pleaded. "This is the last time we can ride through Rome at midnight in an open carriage."

"That's right," Nan said. "This is our fourth night in Rome—and there's one thing we haven't done yet."

"What?" the boy asked.

"We've got to throw a coin in the Trevi Fountain so that one day we'll return to Rome."

The trio sat in silence as the carriage rolled along the old streets. Jack glanced at Nan as her shoulders stiffened beneath his arm when the lovely fountain came into view.

The carriage eased to a stop and the friends climbed out. Gazing quietly at the stately figure of Neptune on a winged chariot, Leslie said, "I wish I'd brought Mother and Rowley here before they left today. But the three of us will come back to Rome. It's not so far from Paris." Her blonde hair shimmering in the moonlight, she turned to Nan impulsively. "It's so wonderful the way things worked out. I owe it all to you."

Nan started to protest, but Leslie continued, "Oh yes, I do! If it hadn't been for you, I wouldn't have opened that letter in Avignon. Then when you disappeared in Naples, I called and called until I found Rowley, and he and Mother came right away. Nan, he was wonderful! He worked night and day trying to find you."

"I'm glad it all came out right," Nan replied. But her friends heard the note of distress in her voice.

Leslie asked softly, "A little let down since your parents left?"

She looked up, startled. "Oh no. It was great to have them here, but they needed to get back to their work." She hesitated, then said, "It's just that I feel sorry for Mrs. Royston."

"Sorry!" Leslie repeated in astonishment. "How can you feel sorry for that monster?"

"I didn't until the very end," Nan said. "Until she cried."

Jack nodded. "I understand." He paused. "I found out some more about her. She's just what she claimed to be—a schoolteacher on a sabbatical. The CIA thinks she was just a minor agent, never doing anything active for the Communists. When they decided to plant a fake spy in Yugoslavia, the Communists needed someone completely respectable. You can imagine how exciting and romantic it all seemed when she was offered the job. And I guess she felt that way until her confederate tried to run us down. When it was all over, you stood there and she saw the horror of it all."

"Has it spoiled Rome for you?" Leslie asked.

Nan lifted her head and turned to look down the street where a Fiat had skidded to a stop. Moonlight traced soft shadows on the pavement. Then she saw a boy and girl walking hand in hand, oblivious to the rest of the world. Nan smiled, freed from the nightmarish memory of the roaring car. Facing the glistening fountain again, she said, "Of course not. I'll always remember Rome for its beauty."

Nan reached into her purse. She clutched the bright coin for a moment, then swung her arm in a wide arc. The coin gleamed in the moonlight as it flashed through the air to fall softly into the water.

ABOUT THE AUTHOR

Carolyn Hart, an accomplished master of mystery, is the author of twenty previous Death on Demand novels. Her books have won multiple Agatha, Anthony, and Macavity Awards. She is also the creator of the Henrie O series which features a retired reporter, and the Bailey Ruth series which stars an impetuous, redheaded ghost. One of the founders of Sisters in Crime, Hart lives in Oklahoma City.

www.ingramcontent.com/pod-product-compliance
Lightning Source LLC
LaVergne TN
LVHW090607110826
845146LV00001B/292

* 9 7 9 8 3 3 7 2 0 3 9 5 9 *